PRAISE FOR
DAUGHTERS OF LONG REACH

2018 Next Generation Indie Book Awards Winner

I actually read the novel in one day, unable to stop reading. Irene writes great dialogue, which is something I always admire, because it is not easy to do.

—*George Smith, columnist*

American poet Walt Whitman (1819–1892) once wrote: "As soon as histories are properly told there is no need of romances." But Bath author Irene Drago might prove him wrong...This is a shipbuilding, seafaring, family love story, folding in real history and real people, with thoughtful fiction to fill out this clever tale.

—*Bill Bushnell, literary critic/columnist: "Bushnell on Books"*

I loved it! What a fine line you managed.

—*Nanette Gionfriddo, owner of Beyond the Sea*

Drago delivers a beautifully written debut novel set in the town of Bath, nestled along the coast of Maine. The story, steeped in local maritime history, deftly weaves past and present honoring core New England values—love of family, love of history, and the importance of fighting for what you believe. Readers will be well pleased!

—*Julie Shea, owner of The Mustard Seed Bookstore*

DAUGHTERS
OF **LONG REACH**

Maine tides bring a family home

For Jane,
Reach for love!

IRENE M. DRAGO

Irene M. Drago

2019

Cover Art
Claudette Gamache, PSA, MCIAPS

Cover Design
Amy Files

Designed and produced by
Maine Authors Publishing
12 High Street, Thomaston, Maine 04861
www.maineauthorspublishing.com

Printed in the United States of America

For my dad,
Chief Petty Officer Francis Donald Murtagh,
who taught me how to be brave
and how to tell a story from the heart.

ACKNOWLEDGMENTS

I would never have completed this novel without the help of family and friends, including the artists and historians I met along the way. I am deeply thankful to the following: my husband, Joe Drago, who read all of my drafts and kept loving me through the whole writing process. My friends Joanne Marco, Kathy Sullivan, and Megan Shea, who all agreed to read my second draft and provided me with valuable feedback and encouragement. My friends at Sagadahoc Preservation, Inc., especially Lorena Coffin, Judy Barrington, and Tracy LaMaestra, who helped me research the history of our house in Bath. My cover artist and dear friend, Claudette Gamache. A rare and beautiful spirit, Abby France-McEntee, who read my second-to-last draft and gave me some brilliant advice. The library staffs at the Patten Free Library and the Maine Maritime Museum, who generously answered my questions. Hoagy Bix Carmichael, who gave me permission to use the words to his father's song, "Ole Buttermilk Sky," which he wrote with lyricist Jack Brooks in 1946. My skilled editors, Jane Eklund and Genie Daley. My publisher, Maine Authors Publishing, who guided me to the finish line!

PROLOGUE

If my mother were alive today, I would ask her a lot of important questions that I never had a chance to ask. I would ask her why she never returned to Maine to live. I know she was born in Maine because she talked about it a lot when I was a little girl growing up near the Brooklyn Navy Yard. My mom loved to tell stories about playing on Popham Beach, walking out to Fox Island at low tide, and taking ferry rides across the Kennebec River. Sadly, my parents and I only spent one summer vacation in Maine. I was fourteen years old, and we stayed at the Sebasco Lodge. My mom told me it was one of Eleanor Roosevelt's favorite places to rusticate. We took a boat ride from Fort Popham to Seguin Island and hiked up a winding trail, flanked by wildflowers, to the historic lighthouse standing guard over the harbor. Sunbeams drenched our path, so we didn't encounter any restless spirits from the other side, but the friendly lighthouse keeper told us about the ghosts that haunted the island, and I was genuinely shocked by every word he said.

During that magical summer, we visited Bath's storybook library on numerous occasions. It looked like a castle on a hill, and it had an old ship's cannon on its north-side lawn. My dad took a picture of me sitting on that cannon. I still have it. On the Fourth of July, we spread a blanket on the hill and watched the fireworks light up the Kennebec. A few days later, we went on a guided tour of Bath Iron Works. My mom and dad seemed so happy to be surrounded by maritime history. Their obvious delight in everything nautical made them seem younger and way more fun-loving. More than anything else, I remember the sparkle in my mother's hazel eyes. Unfortunately, by the time I was sixteen, that sparkle was gone. Cancer isn't the only disease that strikes good people. There are others, and one of them found my mother. In a blink, she disappeared.

I believe Juliet, in William Shakespeare's *Romeo and Juliet*, was wrong when she opined, "What's in a name? That which we call a rose by any other name would smell as sweet." My mother, Stella Rose Donovan, was the essence of beauty, the star in a garden of summer roses, and I don't think any other name would have captured her spirit as well.

I was seventeen years old when my mother's soul left her broken body and sailed away in search of a harbor free from pain. Her passing left a hole in my heart that I have never been able to fill. On sky-blue days, I like to imagine that my mother's heavenly harbor is Long Reach. That's the four-mile stretch along the Kennebec River in Bath, Maine, that she told me about almost every night at bedtime. She had so many stories to tell about shipbuilders, sea captains, shanty songs, and tall ships. I asked her one night why she had left Bath, and she answered with smiling eyes, "I fell in love with a handsome navy man with broad shoulders and a big smile, and I decided to follow him." (If I could have one more conversation with my mother, I would insist on more details.)

In the 1960s, hardly anyone knew the name of my mother's killer, lupus erythematosus. It was a new term in the medical journals. Only a select group of specialists were familiar with its symptoms, and they were just developing a course of treatment. It was a long, scary name for a cruel and painful disease. At our brownstone in Brooklyn, lupus was Public Enemy Number One. My dad was at the end of his naval career, and he was rarely home. He was the captain of the USS *Dyess*, which cruised the North Atlantic from Brooklyn to Halifax on a regular basis. After Mom died, the house ran on empty. In fact, I could hear a lonely echo in the entryway every afternoon when I returned from school and shouted "Hi!" in hopes someone would answer. Fifty years later, I remember my mother's soft, honey-sweet voice, and I say her name from time to time because that's how love survives. Lupus did not erase Stella Rose Donovan. Her love is still here.

My mother was a navy nurse. She joined the navy in 1942, one week after her graduation from Lenox Hill Hospital's nursing school. She met my dad, Lt. Commander Francis Donovan, on the USS *Solace*, the hospital ship known by every blue jacket serving in the South Pacific as The Great White Ship. My father had suffered serious burns when his heavy cruiser, the USS *Northampton*, was sunk during the Battle of Tassafaronga at Guadalcanal. Growing up, I heard my dad recount the harrowing story of how the "Fighting Nora" slipped into a black hole while he and the other survivors swam away as fast as they could to escape the flames. By the grace of God, my dad made a full recovery, and he also fell in love with Stella, his gentle nurse with dreamy eyes. They promised to write to each other, and two years later they arranged to spend a few days of liberty together in Hawaii. I was born nine months after that rendezvous on the sands of Waikiki. My mother named me Eleanor—after Eleanor Roosevelt—but my dad started calling me Ellie as soon as he received the telegram with news of my birth.

Shortly after the war ended, my parents were married in San Diego by a navy chaplain. Their marriage was filled with love and a shipload of fun. I only wish my mother had been given more time. She left us before I had a chance to ask her the most important questions, like: "What should I be when I grow up?" "How do you know you're in love?" "What's the best time to start a family?" "Should I take this job?" "Which house is the right one to buy?" "What do you tell your child when someone breaks their heart?" I wonder what her answers would have been.

CHAPTER 1

2013

The sun coming up over Long Reach fills me with hope every morning. In the 1850s, Long Reach was the home of more than twenty shipyards, the key to Bath's glorious maritime history. Early mornings are quieter these days, and just before dawn I like to stand in the middle of our sunroom, which is a hundred yards from the Kennebec River, and look east. If the sky is clear, I can see daybreak, misty rays of gold skimming over the water, and I can read my mother's hand-stitched sampler: "If you tie the sailor's knot tight enough, your ship will survive the storm, and it will bring you home." In life, Stella Rose Donovan was usually right; since her passing, I listen to her words even more.

"Mom, what are you doing up at six o'clock on a Monday morning?"

Anna had come down the back staircase in her bare feet. She was wearing a white sleep shirt that barely reached the top of her knees, and she was trying, unsuccessfully, to push her curly chestnut hair away from her hazel eyes.

I responded in a highly caffeinated voice. "What are you doing up at this hour?"

Anna stretched and answered with a yawn, "I was up all night writing. For some unknown reason, the words were flowing."

"That's the magic of Bath! This city brings out the artist in everyone, especially painters and writers."

"Well, I don't believe in magic, but if last night's productivity continues, I will have to consider the possibility."

"Bath will make you a believer! But to answer your question, I'm up early for a reason. I have to meet my friends at the cemetery to launch our protest."

Anna shook her head in disbelief. "What are you talking about?"

"I told you last week that the bulldozers were going to arrive early Monday morning to dig up Section One of the cemetery. Remember?"

"Yes, vaguely, but what exactly are you planning to do?"

"I'm going to stand at the entrance of the cemetery with at least half a dozen members of Nequasset Preservation, Inc., including Doris Van der Waag, to prevent Maine DOT's crew from passing through the gates."

As I spoke, I could feel my body temperature rise. The Maine Department of Transportation's plan to improve Old Route 1 by widening Beacon Street was an outrage because it called for the destruction of the oldest part of the Beacon Hill Cemetery where many of Bath's founding families were buried. My friend Doris, the president of NPI, had called me weeks before to ask me to join her movement to stop the project, and I had hoped Anna would support the cause, as well. But Anna's lack of interest had surprised me because she clearly admired Doris, a well-connected New York designer who, albeit retired, still maintained an apartment in Manhattan. Despite their significant difference in age, Anna and Doris had liked each other the minute they met. And I was secretly glad that Anna had met a kindred spirit in Bath.

"Would you like to join us? You know how to craft words, and we may need that talent today."

"No, they're predicting rain, and I don't want to be standing under an umbrella when a burly construction worker starts moving dirt around."

"It wouldn't hurt you, Anna, to lean into this fight just a little. Think of it as another way to express your creative energy. Get involved and shout for justice. And who knows, maybe you'll uncover some interesting material for a future screenplay."

"Well said, Mom, but I don't think NPI needs me to save the cemetery. Truth be told, I think you're dreaming the impossible dream. You know Route 1 can't handle all the summer traffic. Let the DOT do its job."

I knew Anna's argument was valid. According to a recent news report, more than 18,000 vehicles accessed the Sagadahoc Bridge from Bath's viaduct on a daily basis during the months of July and August on their way to Damariscotta, Boothbay, and Bar Harbor. The Maine DOT had the right to improve and expand Old Route 1 and Beacon Street to ease traffic. Unfortunately, their plan could erase the names of some of the most important sea captains and shipbuilders in Bath's history by destroying their tombstones.

"Anna, some of the graves on Beacon Hill have been there for more than three hundred years. In my opinion, Section One is a national treasure!"

"Be reasonable, Mom. Sometimes the landscape, like people, has to change."

"Maybe, but all my years of living have taught me that everything changes and everything remains the same. We should honor the men and women who built this city by caring for their final resting place on Beacon Hill."

"Really, Mom! You never cease to amaze me. I'm not the only one in this family searching for a noble purpose. You are always trying to right the wrongs, just like Don Quixote."

"Thirty years of teaching Spanish will do that. You know, the words of Miguel de Cervantes peppered the speeches of Lincoln, Kennedy, and King, so I guess I'm in good company."

"That's a stretch, Mom. And let's not forget, they were all assassinated!"

Anna looked away. She seemed to be studying the robin perched on the railing of our covered deck. Her eyes were wide open now, and she appeared to be scanning the yard, looking for a place to land and hide from the rain, just like the little bird. I took a deep breath. As usual, I was struggling to find the right words to say to my grown-up daughter.

"Anna, I believe your gypsy soul could find a home here in Bath. Don't forget, your grandmother was born on a farm in Sagadahoc County, and you remind me of her. Your grandma left Maine as a young woman, but now that I live here, I can see how it shaped her personality. I don't know why she didn't return. She died too soon. Maybe she ran out of time. But you, my dear, could stay and be happy here."

Anna bit her lip and looked at the floor. Her silence told me she was ready to listen, so I continued.

"I like to think that the Kennebec River flows through all of us—my mother, you and I—and connects us over time and space. It's funny; your dad and I left home to go to college and neither of us returned. First, it was your dad's naval commitment that kept us away, and then it was graduate school. Before we knew it, the homes that our families once owned were sold, and there didn't seem to be anyplace calling us until we found Bath."

I paused and thought about what Ty had said to me when we looked at our house for the first time with a realtor. He told me that the house reminded him of his best childhood memories. I stood on my toes and kissed him, and we stopped looking at houses.

"Mom, I know how you and Dad feel about Bath, but I've spent the last ten years of my life working as an associate producer, trying to become a successful writer. I'm not sure I can get there from here. And I'm not sure I'm ready to give up my dream."

Anna looked back at me with gentle, fawn-like eyes, and said in a soft but serious tone, "I know how much you care, Mom, but you can't fix this. You can't make me happy. Please stop trying. Let's call a truce, and here's what I'll do to help NPI this morning. I'll bring you a scone and a cup of coffee from the Blue Scone Café at ten o'clock and see how you're doing."

"Well, I won't be alone, so bring a half dozen scones and just as many cups of coffee. And don't forget, the members of NPI take their coffee black and their scones with butter!"

"Okay, but try to keep your cool when the state troopers arrive. I don't think I have enough money in the bank to bail you out of jail. Besides, you're supposed to be enjoying retirement, which means you're supposed to be going to yoga class, joining a book club, writing a blog, and planting a garden! You're supposed to be kicking back on the Kennebec!"

"I've been doing all of those things! In case you haven't noticed, I turned our tired backyard into a flower garden. Have you seen the yellow heliopsis? I also planted cone flowers—two new Butterfly Kisses and two pink Double Delights—with three new peonies and one luscious hydrangea. And don't overlook the butter-cream Shasta daisies.

"Okay, Mom. You have a green thumb and a great eye for flowers with ice-cream-flavor names, but Beacon Hill Cemetery is not your secret garden, and bureaucrats and construction crews know how to play rough. Try not to rock the boat too much today."

"Don't worry. I'll wear my life vest!"

And on that note, Anna, the wild gypsy rose, shook

her head and climbed up the back staircase, likely to curl up under the three-hundred-count cotton sheets that she had missed so desperately while she was on the road.

Sometimes I feel as if Anna and I are two sides of the same coin, a typical mother–daughter paradox. Anna is a tall, artsy brunette, and I'm a petite, fiery blonde, but we both cherish family and friends above all else. I also suspect that Anna, like me, yearns to belong. We seek people with open minds and open hearts, but we seek them in different ways. As I grabbed my yellow rain slicker and walked out the door to face the rough-and-tumble construction crew on Beacon Hill, it was my turn to shake my head as I whispered, "Anna, Anna, quite contrary…"

When I got into my blue Subaru and pulled out of the driveway to head north, the drizzle suddenly turned to hard rain, and I quietly said, "Holy crap!" To quiet the rain, I turned on the radio. By the time I reached Beacon Street, The Byrds were singing "Turn! Turn! Turn!" For a fleeting moment my thoughts turned back to a rainy day in 1965 when I was visiting the College of the Holy Cross with my Barnard roommate. My head was down as I walked up the library steps, and I crashed into Tyler J. Malone, the smart and funny political science major from Virginia who would eventually throw a lasso around my heart and pull me close forever. I'm not a poet, but I could definitely feel the rhythm and rhyme of that extraordinary day.

My thoughts drifted. I looked through the window and spied the Chinese Fringe tree that Ty and I often stop to admire on afternoon walks with our dog, Freckles. By the size of its multistemmed trunk, it's probably a hundred and fifty years old or more. When its blooms first opened, Ty thought they looked like pink smoke, and I told him that there were a lot of old, unusual trees along our street because sea captains used to live here, and they often returned from long voyages with exotic trees from faraway places like Shanghai and Calcutta. Ty kidded that going on a walk with me was like taking a history or botany class. Once, he told me that I, not he, should be the college professor. I remember my quick response: "No, Dr. Malone, I'm just a high school teacher."

He responded in a deep, sexy voice, "Never *just*," and I giggled like a schoolgirl because those two words felt like a lingering kiss.

As I approached the cemetery, the rain stopped, and I spied a rainbow over the hill. That's Maine! The weather is ever-changing, and the stunning views are amazing. It's easy to fall in love with Maine. I didn't even try to resist! While helping Doris and other NPI researchers prepare house histories for the historic district, I had come across a book on the shipbuilders of Maine and learned that Maine's first ship was the *Virginia*, built in 1607 at the Popham Colony. Reading about those daring colonists made me think about my family's own naval history and the role destiny plays in our lives. I believe I was destined to meet Ty Malone, a naval officer and a magician, who would turn the impossible into the inevitable. He would take me away from home only to bring me back to a place that would feel more like home than anyplace I had ever known or imagined.

When I was a child, I used to listen to my mother's bedtime stories about tall wooden ships and iron destroyers. On starry nights, my mother would tell me that my father's first command, the USS *Power*, was built at a magical shipyard. That was her favorite story. Now I realize my mother was referring to Bath Iron Works. My father survived Pearl Harbor and every major battle of the Pacific during World War II. Without a doubt, he served on more than one Bath-built destroyer, and a Bath-built ship brought him home. As I grow older, I remember my mother's stories more vividly, and I think they're part of the reason I feel so comfortable in Bath.

I arrived at the cemetery just in time to see a bulldozer moving toward Section One. As soon as I stepped out of my car, I spotted Doris standing at the wrought-iron gates and whispered "Thank God." It was a blessing that one of us was always on time. I hurried up the hill to join her. Our fight was about to begin.

CHAPTER 2

1855

"Charlotte, my dear, I'm afraid helping the Catholics has cost us dearly," said Captain Henry Goss as he stood looking out at the Kennebec from the front door of his stately home on the corner of Washington and Pearl Streets.

"Don't say that, Henry," Charlotte replied from the stairway directly behind him.

"You helped good men and women who care for their children as we care for ours. Their lives, and their skilled hands and bent backs have helped you and others build ships up and down the Kennebec, especially here at Long Reach."

Henry turned to face his petite, chestnut-haired wife. With her tiny frame and fine features, she looked like a young girl, but the bulge beneath her sleeping gown revealed she was a woman with a baby on the way. Perhaps this one would be a girl, but probably not. The Goss family seemed to produce an abundance of tall, strong boys who in turn grew up to be shipmasters and shipbuilders along Long Reach, the section of the Kennebec River known around the world for crafting the best and fastest sailing ships.

When Henry spoke again, he lowered his head as if in prayer. "You're right, Charlotte, but the most disturbing truth is that we could lose the shipyard if we don't increase our profits."

Charlotte knew that her husband and his partner, Ethan Sawyer, were renting a portion of Johnson Rideout's shipyard in hopes of buying it as soon as they could secure a loan. She also knew that they hoped to make an offer for the whole yard in the near future, but she had not known until this minute that her husband feared losing his investors and customers because of his support for the Catholics.

Charlotte's green eyes, always expressive, flashed. "How could this be, and why do you sound so defeated?"

"Some of our most prominent investors have withdrawn their support because we helped the Catholics find a new place to worship after the Know Nothings burned down the Old South Church."

Remembering the heat wave that had stirred everyone's passion the previous summer, Charlotte closed her eyes and shuddered. With her whole heart and soul, she believed that July 6, 1854, would be remembered as one of the darkest days in Bath's history. The Know Nothings referred to themselves as the Native American Party, but they weren't Native Americans. They were simply angry people who wanted to find someone, or some group, to blame for all of their troubles.

She opened her eyes and sighed. "Oh, Henry, why did they have to burn the church?"

"They hate Irish Catholics, and they hate French and German Catholics, too. They hate anyone who thinks or prays differently than they do. By God, I fear they even hate themselves!"

Charlotte was shocked by Henry's choice of words. He was a kind-hearted man who usually didn't put *God*, *fear*, and *hate* in the same sentence. She thought a minute before responding in a calm voice.

"I've read about the Know-Nothing Party. They are stirring up the workers by blaming immigrants for all their woes."

Charlotte doubted that these hateful Know Nothings even knew the history of the region. She, on the other hand, loved to read the old stories about Chief Mowhatawormit, who was called Chief Robert (Robin) Hood by the English because of his clever negotiating style. Charlotte shared those stories with her sons, who were fascinated by the Native Americans. With great attention to detail, Charlotte told them how the Parker family arrived on Roscohegan Island in 1659 and quickly purchased it from Chief Robin Hood and his tribe, the Abenaki. Later, in honor of this historic purchase, the island became known as Parker Island, and even later it was renamed Georgetown by its growing population of transplanted Englishmen. Truthfully, the good, hardworking people of Georgetown and Bath were all immigrants of one kind or another.

Deep in thought, Henry nodded. When he responded, his eyes were fixed on the pumpkin-pine floor. "These political activists are making trouble for all the shipbuilders in Bath. Several crews have refused to show up for work if Catholics are going to be working at the same dock."

He raised his head to look into Charlotte's eyes. On this hot summer day, they looked sea-green, and, as usual, they took his breath away. After six years of marriage, these two strong and caring spirits seemed to function as one. Charlotte wrapped her arms around her husband and hugged him as tightly as she could with their unborn baby kicking within her.

"My dear, don't listen to angry voices. Our friends and neighbors know that you were right to defend the Catholics. I think those hateful arsonists are sad, lonely men looking for someone to bully. You, on the other hand, are good and just. Now, enough of this gloom and doom! I have an idea that will help you and Ethan build your own fleet of ships. Imagine a sign on Front Street that says 'Goss and Sawyer Shipbuilding Company.'"

"You always have a dream in mind!" said Henry with a smile as Charlotte took a short breath before launching into her newest scheme.

"Our house is sitting on a choice piece of land overlooking Long Reach, and from this elevation you can see at least four of Bath's twenty-one shipyards. I cherish this place we call home, but we can move this house to a smaller lot across the street, and we can sell the land it now stands on for a lot of money. I know James Patten has been itching to build a mansion with a river view. I suspect he would buy it for a pretty penny."

"Charlotte, if you were a man I would fear you, but I feel blessed that you're my wife, and I can make love to you every night."

Henry brushed Charlotte's silky hair off of her shoulder and nuzzled her sweet-smelling neck. Then he gently wrapped his big arms around her waist, careful not to squeeze their baby, and lingeringly kissed her soft rosebud mouth. When he was forced to take a breath, he leaned back and made her a promise.

"I'll get David Orr to help. He'll find a good crew of men and strong oxen to move the house. And don't worry—I can build you a new outhouse by myself."

Charlotte kissed his cheek and whispered, "You make the sweetest promises!"

Henry whispered back, "That's because I have such a darling wife. You make me feel like anything is possible. Of course we can move the house! It's a short trip from the west side of Washington Street to the east side."

Charlotte started to shake with laughter, and Henry had to kiss her again to quiet her. Their unborn child could only handle so much excitement in one day!

Later that night, Charlotte woke with a start. She had been feeling the strength of their baby all evening. Falling asleep had been difficult, but this feeling was more cramp-like than kick-like. She recognized the onset of labor immediately. Her oldest son, Jonathan, was already five years old, and Francis was three. Those births had gone smoothly, and she was not worried, but she felt a need to stand up and move about the room to relieve the waves of pain that were quickening now. As she stepped out of bed she suddenly felt wet. There was a circle of water expanding on the floor at her feet, and she knew it was time. Wishing not to alarm Henry, she gently reached over and gave him a nudge.

"Henry," she whispered, "the baby is coming."

As Charlotte turned on the oil lamp near their bed, Henry stirred and tried to bring Charlotte's face into focus. Her words were falling on him like a cold rain.

"Did you say it's time?" he asked in a sleepy voice.

"Yes, wake my mother. Tell her to get the birthing room ready. Try not to wake the boys, but go for my sister, Amy. Mother will need her assistance. Please go quickly. This one is early…" She paused, breathless. "Our baby is coming and won't wait."

Henry noticed the wet floor. He was up and fumbling with his pants as if he had never before donned a pair of pants one leg at a time. He was talking, but his words, like his legs, were stumbling over each other. Finally, he reached Hannah's bedroom at the end of the hall.

"Hannah!"

"I'm awake, Henry. I've been waiting. Go! I will take care of Charlotte and the baby."

Hannah Riggs, born on Georgetown Island in 1794, was famous for her intuition. Her family and friends always sought her opinion and sage advice. If Hannah felt something was going to happen, it usually did. Last night, before retiring, Hannah had felt that the baby would be coming soon, so she had filled a big kettle with water and placed it on the stove. Now she hurried to the kitchen to light the stove and took a basin out of the cupboard. She had already placed the necessary sheets in the birthing room.

Minutes later, as Hannah was heading up the back staircase with the filled basin, she heard Charlotte's first loud gasp of pain. Hannah's small feet were deftly quick on the narrow stairs, and within seconds she entered the birthing room to see Charlotte standing by the bed, bent at the waist with one hand on the bedpost. Hannah's maternal instincts took control of the moment. Charlotte was in good hands.

By the time Henry returned home with Amy, Jonathan and Francis were sitting at the top of the staircase, only a few steps away from the birthing room door. As soon as Henry saw their tear-stained faces, he knew they had been listening to their mother's screams, and he rushed up the stairs to console them, with Amy close behind. As Henry lifted little Francis up into his strong arms, Jonathan buried his face in Amy's skirt. In a tender voice, Amy tried to reassure them.

"Let me go help your mother," Amy said. "Be brave. I'll be back in no time with your new little brother or sister."

Amy turned and entered the birthing room. Less than an hour later, a new baby's cry could be heard ringing from the upstairs room. It was a boy! True to her word, Aunt Amy stepped out into the hallway to introduce Jonathan and Francis to their brother, Thomas. July 13, 1855, was turning out to be a glorious day, and it was only eight o'clock in the morning.

CHAPTER 3

2013

Anna pulled off her hood and shivered a little as she stepped out of the rain and into the Blue Scone Café. "So what will it be today, Ms. Malone?" asked Nick in a booming voice.

"Six coffees, five blueberry scones, and one apricot to go, please."

Nick shook his head and chuckled. "That's a big order. Who prefers apricot?"

Anna answered with a wink. "Doris Van der Waag prefers apricot scones, and I try to please her because she has exquisite taste."

"And where are you going with all of this sugar and caffeine?"

Anna smiled. "I could tell you, but then I'd have to—"

"Stop! I don't need to know. Just be careful driving around with all that hot coffee."

Anna skillfully held a cardboard tray with six coffees in one hand and a bag of scones in the other hand as she pushed the café door open with her hip.

"Thanks, Nick! I'll be back soon!"

"I bet you will!" shouted Nick with a wave.

When Anna arrived at the cemetery, she realized the challenge of the day would be finding a place to park. There was a line of cars from the wrought-iron gates to the five-way intersection, but thanks to Anna's great parking karma, she found a spot behind Doris's vintage Volvo wagon. As she maneuvered into the space, she remembered the first time she had seen Doris at NYU. Anna was a junior then, and Doris had been invited by the school of theater to give a lecture on set design. Needless to say, she left an indelible impression. Anna thought her designs were revolutionary. And when Anna met Doris again in Bath, she said, "You probably don't remember me, but I attended one of your lectures at NYU. And by the way, I think you're Debra Kerr's doppelgänger."

Doris immediately connected Debra Kerr with *An Affair to Remember* and *The King and I*, and she tipped her stylish hat and humbly said thank you. For Anna, meeting Doris in Bath was like finding a bit of hope.

Since graduating from NYU, Anna had been working behind the scenes on highly charged movie sets, but had recently stopped. She had worked hard to be noticed in the industry and to earn a credit at the end of a film, but someone had robbed her of that prize and derailed her dream. As an aspiring screenwriter, she had carried a small notebook around and jotted down random ideas and observations for future projects. And sometimes, while waiting in a restaurant or sitting on a park bench, she would sketch a person or a scene that fit a story line she hoped to develop, but she had stopped doing that, too. She had packed up all of her notebooks and sketch pads with no intention of ever opening them again. Then last night she'd had a change of heart. She unpacked the box, and one of her sketches had sparked an idea, and she wrote all night long.

Walking up the hill to the entrance of the cemetery, Anna couldn't help but think that her years as an associate producer seemed like a lifetime ago. Life wasn't working out as she had planned, but at least she was meeting some genuine artists on the mid-coast of Maine. They weren't deceitful and manipulative like some of the people she had worked for in Hollywood. Doris's voice was like a breath of fresh air. She found her ideas and her energy inspiring. And Doris wasn't the only artist in town. Who knew that Bath would be a hangout for so many gifted people? If she let herself, she could almost imagine being happy here.

Anna passed through the gates of the cemetery just in time to see a photographer from the *Daily Times Record* snap a picture of Doris and Ellie as they raised roughly made signs and shouted, "Don't Tread on the Dead!" Anna shook her head in amazement and whispered under her breath, "Here we go." Her eyes scanned the crowd, and then she called out, "Hey, Mom, I've brought scones!"

* * *

In a chorus of a hundred people, I could always hear Anna's Irish-coffee voice, warm and stimulating. Today, there were only half a dozen people assembled at the cemetery gates, so I heard Anna clear as a bell, and I stopped chanting "Don't Tread on the Dead!" long enough to look and wave. She was dressed in her signature purple T-shirt, yoga pants, and white sneakers, and her hair was tied back in the usual ponytail. In her left hand was a bag of scones, and in her right hand she was balancing a cardboard tray with steaming cups of coffee. By the time she reached us, she was slightly out of breath and wet all over from the soaking rain. Doris and I laughed when she handed us our care package, and she responded with an upbeat smile.

"Happy Monday morning, ladies! I've come with your ten o'clock coffee. It's time for all the revolutionary Bathites to take a break."

"Anna Rose Malone, don't be cute. We're trying to make some noise so DOT sends over one of their big chiefs to meet with us. The media has already arrived, and they're ready to tell our side of the story. Now we just have to get the city and state officials to listen."

"Well, that's great, but I also see a bunch of police cars and state troopers over there as well. Someone could get hurt. I'm thinking about the construction workers, of course. The preservationists will be fine!"

Anna helped pass out the coffee and scones as she expressed her concern. Clearly, all the hoopla was making her nervous, and she was worried about legal repercussions. I could tell she was trying to defuse the situation.

"Mom, your favorite expression is 'Let freedom ring!' Maybe some people in Maine feel the expansion of Beacon Street will prevent annoying traffic jams. People are free to think differently, aren't they?"

Before I could answer, Anna turned to leave. She moved so quickly that she didn't realize someone from DOT was standing directly behind her, but I did, and I watched as she collided with a handsome man in a hard hat who was clearly the chief engineer, Jake Summers. I had looked him up online the night before. According to one of the articles I found, he was a veteran and had survived two tours in Iraq before attending Worcester Polytechnic Institute in Massachusetts on the GI Bill. I also found out that he grew up in Wiscasset, Maine. The article said that his father owned the only auto repair shop in that quaint little village, which means he probably worked under the hood of every car in a fifty-mile radius before graduating from high school. After 9/11, he enlisted in the Marine Corps, and the military put his skills to good use. He spent most of his first tour repairing Humvees in the desert instead of searching for insurgents, and that probably saved his life, but he didn't escape the war without injury. He was wounded during his second tour and received a Purple Heart.

* * *

As soon as Jake saw Anna's curves in her purple T-shirt, he wondered if she would like to see the sketches of kayaks and canoes on his bedroom wall. He knew his chances were good because most women found him attractive, but there was something about her eyes that stopped him from being too confident—and then his thoughts were interrupted by Anna's soft-spoken words.

"Oh, I'm sorry. I didn't see you."

"No worries. We're still standing."

Anna noticed Jake's hand was touching her shoulder, and she could feel his bicep pressing against her. Suddenly, she wanted to flirt.

"Did you say 'we'? Do I know you?"

Jake laughed. "No, you don't know me, but I'm not wrong about us. And for the record, you bumped into me when I was standing still."

Anna said, "Ouch!" and stepped back to offer Jake her hand. "I'm Anna Malone."

As they shook hands, Jake replied in the lowest voice he could muster, "I'm Jake Summers, and I'm glad we bumped into each other."

Anna smiled. "There's that 'we' again."

Before Jake could say another word, Doris shouted over from the picket line twenty feet away. "Excuse me, sir, but are you in charge of the crew operating all that heavy machinery over there?"

"Yes, I'm the chief engineer," Jake called back.

Anna gave Doris a stop-now look, and then she looked back at Jake with a terrified expression. She put her hand on his shoulder and softly said, "Run! Run now! There's nothing you can do to escape their fury!"

Anna walked away. When Jake glanced over his shoulder to watch her ponytail bounce, everyone on the hill knew that he was smitten.

* * *

When I was teaching at Laurel High School, I witnessed more than a few love-at-first-sight moments, but I had never seen Cupid's arrow strike my own daughter. In Spanish class, it was called *un flechazo*. Who knew you could find magic in an old, soon-to-be-demolished cemetery? Anna walked away as if she were floating, and I could see Jake's heart pounding through his polo shirt! The fight to save Beacon Hill was about to begin, and Doris, Jake, Anna, and I were going to be in the middle of it.

"Ellie!"

"Yes, I'm here, Doris. You don't have to shout."

"See that tall young man with the sunburned nose over there?"

I answered with a nod, and she kept talking.

"He looks like a Greek god. But Greek god or not, we have to talk with him."

"That's Jake Summers, the DOT engineer."

Doris raised an eyebrow, and I countered with a shrug.

"I looked him up online. And yes, we should go over there and meet him. It's the least we can do in the name of preservation."

As we walked toward Jake, I wanted to laugh—but I didn't because Doris was ready to step into the ring. She was going to tell Jake that he and his crew were about to tear up one of the most historic graveyards in Maine. And then, like a one-two punch, I was going to insist that they stop work immediately.

"Hello, Mr. Summers. I'm Doris Van der Waag, the president of NPI, and this is Ellie Malone, one of our chairpersons. We're here to stop this travesty. You are about to destroy the graves of some of Bath's most prominent sea captains and shipbuilders."

"Please," I added, "tell your men to turn off their heavy machinery. Don't disturb the peace of this sacred ground for the sake of a wider street."

"Good morning, ladies." Jake Summers said with

a smile. "Okay; I'm in charge of this project, but unfortunately, I'm also the harbinger of bad news. Bath's City Council has already met and approved the project. I'm not here to argue. I'm just doing my job."

I could see Doris's shoulders square off and her back straighten, so I decided to jump in before Doris said something she would regret.

"We're aware of the council's decision, but it doesn't reflect our city's commitment to historic preservation. I'm sure the council believed it was voting in Bath's best interests, but the project's impact on the cemetery wasn't thoroughly discussed. Please stop and take some time to consider our objection."

"Well said. Is it Mrs. Malone?" Jake asked politely.

"Yes, Ellie Malone. I'm the mother of that lovely brunette you were flirting with a moment ago."

Jake paused, and then he responded in a more serious tone.

"I was being friendly, not flirtatious. But right now I think we have to focus on the problem at hand. I am employed by the State of Maine, and I have been directed by the Department of Transportation to begin exhuming this part of the cemetery."

For Doris, those were fighting words. "Sir, this is not our first time at the rodeo! I have a degree in historical preservation from Colombia University, and Ellie graduated with honors from Barnard. We know what we're talking about, and you should listen!"

* * *

Jake took a moment to scan the crowd assembled at the entrance of the cemetery. His instincts told him that these two articulate women were right, but he hadn't survived two tours of desert warfare in Iraq to fail in Maine. He took a deep breath, reached his hand slowly into his pocket and pulled out his cell phone.

"Sir, we have a situation on Beacon Street. Since

there's a group of both protesters and press here, I suggest we postpone digging. We can put up fencing around the construction site and shield the trees we hope to save, but that's all we can reasonably do today without creating a media frenzy."

Jake listened to the director's heated reply, and then he calmly added, "Sir, I think we need to speak with the head of Bath's City Council and lay out a definitive plan for relocating the graves in Section One. Mrs. Doris Van der Waag and Mrs. Ellie Malone are standing in front of me, sir, and they have reminded me that Bath is the City of Ships, and there are more than a few sea captains buried on this hill. They strongly feel it is the community's duty to preserve those graves."

* * *

Doris and I listened to Jake's response, and Doris turned and whispered, "I guess you can't judge a man by his hard hat. Maybe this tin man has a heart after all."

I laughed and whispered back, "I think we just won our first battle."

CHAPTER 4

1860

Upstairs, Charlotte was writing another letter to Henry. She was seated at a small desk near the east-facing window because it offered her the best view of the river. Thanks to Henry's master carpenter and his crew, their house had been moved across the street to its present location near Cedar Street in January of 1856. One ox was injured while pulling the house on a large sleigh, but none of the men were hurt, and the house was none the worse for its short journey. Now, Charlotte's pen was poised over a blank sheet of paper as she gazed at the three-masted schooner under construction just beyond her backyard. If only business had been a little better, perhaps Henry and his partner could have hired a captain to command the *Roanoke* on its passage around Cape Horn to San Francisco. Henry had already been gone for three months. Today, with help from her mother and two sisters, they had celebrated Thomas's fifth birthday, and Henry was absent.

As soon as Henry had announced that he would

have to sail with the *Roanoke*, Charlotte decided to convert the back bedroom into a quiet writing place. It was a good decision because every afternoon when the boys had their quiet time, Charlotte could retreat to the writing nook and "talk with Henry." Without this daily practice, she feared they would grow apart and become strangers.

"Henry, my love," she began to write in a beautiful, flowing script that Henry would savor reading over and over again whenever the letters caught up to him—in Charleston, Valparaiso, San Francisco, or in port in Formosa. The voyages were long and dangerous, but that was to be expected. Before their children arrived, Charlotte had sailed with Henry on one of his many passages around Cape Horn. But after observing the deadly diseases that could plague a ship and keep its crew in quarantine for months, and surviving the heavy gales of a storm at sea, she had decided that she would remain on land as soon as the children came, and she would try to keep them safe until they were old enough to choose their own risks.

Henry, my love,

Today, Thomas turned five, and we celebrated! I wish you could have seen our little boy's face when I gave him a big slice of strawberry shortcake. He grabbed it with both hands, and in a minute his nose, mouth, and chin became as red as the strawberries. Amy managed to sketch his sweet face, and I am enclosing that portrait to pull you home.

I must go and look in on the boys. It's four o'clock here, and that seems to be the howling hour. Jonathan and Francis like to quarrel around this time every afternoon. I can hear their voices right now, and they are definitely agitated. I suspect they miss you as much as I do, but I don't know how that could be possible because I miss you more every hour of every day. Please don't worry about us. We are fine, and we will continue to be fine until you come home safe and unharmed. You remain the captain of my heart.

Forever yours,
Charlotte

P.S. Shortly after Thomas's birthday party ended, I heard him tell Aunt Amy, "Father wanted to come, but he's the captain of a tall ship, and he has to help all of the sailors find their way home."

She sealed her words with a kiss, and left her peaceful nook to settle the ongoing dispute between Jonathan and Francis.

Charlotte arrived at her sons' bedroom door just in time to see feathers fly. Francis had just smacked his older brother's head with a downy-soft pillow, and Jonathan was about to retaliate with his own fluffy weapon when their grandmother caught his arm in midair. How did Hannah move so fast? Charlotte stood back to observe the unfolding drama.

"Grandma!" said Jonathan. "Francis says he is going on a voyage with Father before me, but I told him I was the oldest, and I would be joining Father's crew when I turn thirteen."

"Well, the truth is, you will both have a chance to be a ship's boy, but your first experience at sea will not be on the *Roanoke* because that is your father's ship. When the time is right, you will sail with another captain so you can learn without favoritism how to be Kennebeckers. And do you know what they say about Kennebeckers?" Hannah asked her grandsons.

"I know," answered Jonathan. "Kennebeckers only fear God and Cape Cod."

Fascinated with any story connected to the sea, Francis asked, "Why do they fear Cape Cod, Grandma?"

"Well, Francis, the easterly gales are treacherous

near Cape Cod. Kennebeckers are some of the best mariners in the world, and their skills are tested every time they navigate through Hell's Gate at the mouth of the Kennebec River, but they also understand the risk involved in navigating around Cape Cod."

With bright hazel eyes, little Francis replied in a serious tone, "Grandma, I love it when you talk about the Kennebeckers and their wisky passages."

"And risky they are," said Hannah, emphasizing her *r* and trying not to laugh. She knew Francis struggled with the hard *r* sound, as many young children did, especially those who had an *r* in their names. Hannah smiled as she thought about God's sense of humor, and then she turned to Francis and said, "Now, let's gather some wood and help your mother do some chores around here."

Hannah focused her twinkling eyes—her gift to the family—on her two grandsons, and they nodded their agreement. Sometimes the boys wondered if their grandmother's eyes had the power to see everything. They were certainly as big as a snowy owl's, and they always seemed to be wide open and wise.

Charlotte listened to her mother's voice and thanked God for her calming effect on the boys. Henry would not be returning home for months. As a sea captain's wife, she should be used to sleeping alone and running the household without her husband, but she felt Henry's absence every morning, noon, and night. Once Henry and Ethan had opened their shipyard, she thought Henry would be able to stay home and supervise the construction of new square-riggers, but several contracts had been suspended due to the growing fear of war between the North and the South, and Henry had been forced to take command of the *Roanoke* himself, just to make ends meet.

When the boys had left the room, Hannah turned to face her daughter. "Have you finished your letter to Henry?"

"Yes, I will mail it tomorrow morning," Charlotte answered.

Hannah hesitated a moment before inquiring further, "Do you think any of your letters actually reach him?"

"Oh, Mother, of course they do. I wouldn't write them if I didn't believe they would reach him. When I gave birth to Francis, Henry was captain of the *Florence Nightingale*, and he was at sea. Several months later, while he was on a passage from Acapulco to Tacoma, his ship encountered another Yankee vessel that was carrying mail. Upon arriving home, he showed me a stack of letters tied together with blue ribbon. That was the ribbon I sent him to announce the happy delivery of our baby boy!"

Hannah reached out and gently touched her daughter's hand. "Honestly, Charlotte, your strength amazes me."

"Why does it surprise you?" Charlotte asked. But before her mother could respond, she stated the obvious. "I'm just like you."

"No, I never had to endure long separations from your father. Our family store was open six days a week, and your father worked from sunrise to sunset, but he was always home for supper. Henry has been away for months on end. It is harder for you..."

Hannah's voice seemed to fade away into sadness as she thought about her daughter's daily struggle to be both mother and father to her three sons while their father performed his duties half a world away.

Hearing her mother's words, Charlotte stood a little taller. And with all the courage she could muster, she smiled.

"I knew when I married Henry that he was a Kennebecker, and he needed to be on the deck of a ship to be fully alive. There's a new term that's being used to describe shipmasters and shipbuilders from New England—Live Yankees—and it suits Henry perfectly. My husband is a mariner, not a merchant, and I accept that truth. In fact, I love him for it."

Hannah wrapped her arms around her strong-minded daughter and said, "I know you do, so why don't you take a stroll down to the post office and mail that letter this afternoon? There's no reason to wait until tomorrow."

CHAPTER 5

1861

Six months later in San Francisco, on January 6, 1861, Captain Robert McGowan, one of the most senior captains in the Trufant and Drummond fleet, picked up a bag of mail intended for his crew and other seamen from Bath. Charlotte's letter was in that bag, along with a letter that her youngest sister had written to Henry a month later. Captain McGowan's ship, the *Ellie*, left the port of San Francisco for the last passage of its long voyage home the next day.

Almost four months later, off the southeastern coast of China, between Formosa and the Bashee Isles, Henry stood outside his cabin and looked out on the vast Pacific Ocean. Before he even lifted his spyglass, he spotted the *Ellie*. Ironically, at almost the same moment, Captain McGowan spied the *Roanoke*. It seemed that destiny was bringing these two wooden sailing ships from Bath together. When Captain McGowan's first officer had distributed the mail among the *Ellie's* crew back in San Francisco, he'd noticed several letters addressed to Captain Henry Goss, a well-known captain who had previously commanded the brig *Florence Nightingale* out of Boston, as well as several Trufant and Drummond ships over the last ten years. The officer immediately alerted Captain McGowan about the letters and the fact that one was marked URGENT. Consequently, as soon as Robert spotted Henry's ship, he ordered his signalman to hoist the flag to request permission to board.

Henry and his crew were excited to see fellow sailors from New England so far from home. When Captain McGowan and several members of his crew climbed aboard, they were greeted with strong handshakes and big smiles. Henry recognized Robert, his old mentor, instantly, and was quick to invite him into his cabin for a drink. After briefly discussing all the nautical news they had to share, Robert took the two letters he had in his breast pocket and handed them to Henry.

"Henry," Robert said, "these letters for you were delivered to my ship in San Francisco, and one of them, as you can see, is urgent. I sincerely hope I am not the bearer of bad news."

Henry held both envelopes in his hand. He did not recognize the handwriting on the one marked URGENT, but he did recognize his wife's beautiful script on the other, and he would have preferred to read that letter first, but under the circumstances, he quickly tore open the urgent letter. His eyes immediately fell to the signature, and he was surprised to see his sister-in-law's name, Emma Riggs. Emma was only seventeen years old, and she was far too absorbed in the drama of her own social life to write her sister's husband at sea. Realizing this was out of character for Emma, Henry was instantly worried as he noticed the date, August 4, 1860, and began to read the single paragraph on the thin sheet of white paper.

Dear Henry,

My heart is heavy as I write you with the news of the illness that has struck Bath and your family. Jonathan and Francis are both gravely ill, and Charlotte and Mother are caring for them day and night at your home. So far, Thomas has been spared thanks to Charlotte's quick thinking. As soon as Jonathan and Francis became sick with high fevers and chills, she told Amy to bring Thomas here to Robinhood Cove and to remain here until this horrible wave of consumption had passed. Amy agreed to bring him, but then she immediately returned to Bath to help nurse the many who have fallen ill. It has been two weeks since Thomas arrived, and he and I remain well, but the doctor sent word yesterday that Hannah now has a high fever and the boys have grown even worse. Charlotte would not want me to worry you, but I fear the situation is dire. Please come home, Henry. Come as fast as you can.

With affection,
Emma

As Henry read Emma's plea, his right hand began to tremble and all the color drained from his face. When he looked up, his eyes were moist, but he did not let himself cry. Instead, he spoke in a deep, low voice.

"I must prepare my crew and my ship for my swift departure. Can I sail with you on the final passage of your voyage back to Bath? The *Roanoke* must complete two more passages before returning home, and I cannot wait. Two of my sons are gravely ill. This letter is from their Aunt Emma, who is now caring for my youngest son in Georgetown. I fear my wife may fall ill as well because her mother has already come down with a high fever."

Captain McGowan immediately agreed to carry his fellow Kennebecker home on the *Ellie*, another Bath-built ship, which had been launched from the Trufant and Drummond shipyard in 1858. His only regret was that he couldn't do more for the young father who was anxious to reach his family before it was too late.

Rubbing his chin, Robert asked, "Who's your first officer? And is he ready to take command?"

"Nathan Rideout is our first officer," said Henry briskly. "He's young, but he's capable."

Robert looked surprised. "Johnson Rideout's son?"

"Yes, that's right. And he's almost as good as his dad!"

Master shipbuilder Johnson Rideout had wanted his youngest son to gain experience at sea by sailing with a captain who was not a Rideout. Since Henry and his partner were renting a portion of the Rideout Shipyard in hopes of becoming master builders, it seemed logical to ask Henry to take Nathan on his next voyage. Now, as fate would have it, Nathan Rideout was about to take command of the *Roanoke* and attempt to fulfill its contract by completing its two remaining passages before sailing home. He was only twenty-four years old.

Within the hour, Captain Goss climbed down from his thousand-ton square-rigger and into a small skiff to bounce across a half nautical mile to reach Captain McGowan's ship. Minutes later, standing on the deck of the *Ellie*, he watched the *Roanoke* sail away toward the horizon.

CHAPTER 6

2013

When I entered the side door, Anna was sitting at the kitchen table, scrolling through e-mails on her laptop, sipping a cup of herbal tea, and waiting for me. I could tell she was anxious to hear about the happenings on Beacon Hill, and I suspected she was eager to hear more about that tall engineer with the piercing blue eyes and Adonis shoulders.

"How did it go?" asked Anna without looking up, and trying not to sound too interested.

As I sat down to pull off my knee-high orange rain boots, I coyly answered, "It went well."

"Okay, Mom, you have my full attention. You know I want to hear all the details, especially those pertaining to Mr. Summers."

"He's a handsome man, isn't he?"

"Yes, he is tall, blond, and handsome," said Anna in a matter-of-fact way. "But this whole crusade against Maine DOT is starting to remind me of *Cool Hand Luke*."

"I don't see the connection."

Anna folded her arms and leaned back in her chair. And then, in a husky voice, she said, "What we have here is a failure to communicate."

I laughed out loud. "And what part would Jake Summers play in that film?"

"He'd be Luke. You know, Paul Newman's part. Did you see those blue eyes? They're *profoundly* blue!"

I stood speechless for a moment in the middle of the kitchen wondering where my cynical daughter had gone, and then I responded, "So you like his eyes, and you think he's a misunderstood prisoner trapped on a chain gang?"

"Very funny, Mom. I'm just saying he seems like a good guy in a bad situation."

"He is. Doris and I believe we have found our superhero in Jake Summers."

Anna threw her hands up. "Do you really think that a DOT engineer is going to help you change the minds of all the councilmen who voted in favor of bulldozing the cemetery in order to widen the state road?"

"When did you stop believing in happy endings, Anna? Don't you believe there's a Don Quixote, or a Lone Ranger, or a Captain America out there who can save the day? Where did all of your cock-eyed optimism go?"

As soon as the words left my mouth, I wanted to take them back. Anna was silent. It was no secret that her career had stopped rather abruptly. After graduating from NYU, she had worked as a production assistant on a local talk show, and then at a New York–based soap opera, and that's where she met Ben Timmons, a producer who offered her a job on a film he was making in Southern California. When that project was completed, Ben hired her for several others.

But Anna had always dreamed of writing the next Great American Novel. When she was working in New York, she kept that dream alive by writing every night. As soon as she moved to LA, her focus narrowed to screenplays, and that ignited her talent, but she was not prepared for the ugly side of Hollywood. She discovered that making movies was a lonely business. My daughter reminded me of my mother's old saying, "You can be lucky at work or lucky in love, but it's hard to be lucky in both." As an artist, Anna was fearless, and she loved to observe people in new and exotic places, but there was also another side to our wild gypsy rose, and that side yearned for a home.

I was lost in thought when I suddenly heard my name.

"Ellie? Can you hear me?"

Anna was calling me by my first name. She only did that when she needed to talk to me and my mind seemed to be somewhere else.

"Sorry," I said. "I was just thinking about—"

"Let me guess. You were thinking about Ben and how he ruined my life."

"No..." I stopped and started again. "I was just thinking about how long it's been since you've shown any interest in a man, or even commented on how attractive they can be. Okay, maybe I was thinking about that narcissist. But for the record, I'm glad he's gone."

"Well, I'm glad we put the period at the end of that statement. Honestly, Mom, I'm over it. Let's not talk about him anymore. Let's talk about now. I'm writing again!"

"I've noticed!" And then I sat down ready to listen.

"I feel like Bath is reviving my creative voice, and my writing is on fire. Maybe it's even restoring my faith in love and romance. I'm not quite sure what's happening, but it feels good."

Anna's enthusiasm surprised me, and all I could say was, "Great!" Then I waited for more good news.

Anna looked at me. Her eyes were smiling. "You know what I love most about Bath?"

"What?"

"It feels real. It feels real to me, like no other place has ever felt. Does that sound crazy?"

"No, I feel that connection, too. Even though we only moved here a few years ago, it feels as if we've always been here, or at least some part of us has always been here."

Anna looked out the window toward the Kennebec. "Maybe it's because we moved around so much. I mean, I was born in San Diego, and then we moved to Charlottesville when Dad was working on his PhD at UVA, and then we moved to DC when he was doing his post doc at Georgetown, and then we moved to Baltimore when he started teaching at Loyola, and then I moved to New York." Anna looked down and swallowed hard. "I think I've lived in too many places."

"Anna Rose, you never cease to amaze me. We don't always agree, but today we're on the same page. Like you, I've been searching for home, and I think I've found it. Bath feels good in so many ways. I heard a song on the radio yesterday about coming home, and the lyrics kept repeating in my head all day long."

"I'm not surprised, Mom. Before 'playlist' was a thing, you had a list of songs for every occasion."

"My mother loved to sing. I remember her singing as she sat by our kitchen window, pulling in the clothesline and unpinning our clean laundry one item at a time. Our neighbors used to open their windows just to listen. They called her the Brooklyn nightingale. I can't sing like your grandma, but I remember the words to all of her favorite songs. Whenever I'm feeling lost or confused, I play those songs in my head, and the music and lyrics seem to guide me. I can still hear her lilting voice."

Anna stood up and walked over to the kitchen sink to rinse out her cup. As she looked out on the garden, she continued our mother–daughter chat.

"Look, it's going to be another beautiful day in Maine. All of this good Maine air is going to clear my head, and I'm going to figure out where I'm going and what I should do when I get there."

Our chat was interrupted when the phone rang. Anna answered.

"Hello, Anna Malone speaking."

I listened while Anna responded to the speaker with a light, happy voice.

"Well, that's a win for NPI. My mom is sitting right here, so you can tell her all the details."

Before handing me the phone, Anna added one more comment. "Doris, you know I'll be there tonight to support the cause."

Now it was Anna's turn to sit and listen.

A few minutes later, I put the phone down and winked at Anna. "Let the games begin!"

Anna laughed. "Sometimes you scare me, Mom. What did Doris say?"

"The chair of the City Council is calling an emergency meeting. He's inviting community leaders to express their concern about Section One. Doris is going to speak, but she wants me to be ready, too."

"Congratulations! It looks like your protest this morning has sparked a dialogue!"

"Thank you, honey. I'm going upstairs to change and put on some makeup. The meeting starts at six o'clock."

Anna shook her head and laughed again. "Uh-oh. I think that means you're putting on your war paint."

"That's right. My mother always told me, 'When you go out to face the world, put some lipstick.' Tonight I'm wearing red, and I'm dressing for success. I think you should, too. I bet that Jake Summers will be there. If I were you, I'd put on that moss-green blouse and those breezy white pants."

"And what color lipstick?" Anna tossed back with a grin.

"Tangerine, of course! You'll be irresistible. And we may need the diversion!"

"Mom! You're unbelievable!" said Anna as she stood up and followed me upstairs.

It was certainly turning out to be a promising day. I couldn't help but wonder what the night would bring, and I wished Ty could be with us. Even though I'd chosen to retire, Ty was still teaching at Loyola, and he was commuting between Baltimore and Bath on a regular basis. This chapter of our life was beginning to resemble our newlywed days when Ty was a lieutenant in the navy, fulfilling his NROTC commitment. Even though a house in Maine and a condo in Baltimore made sense on paper, life was better when Ty was near. I'd welcomed Anna's decision to move home, if only for a little while, and I was delighted she wanted to go to the meeting with me. Of course, I suspected she was more interested in seeing "the guy" than hearing about local politics, but her motive didn't affect my mood. We decided to leave the house a little early so we could stop at Kelly's Irish Pub for a light dinner. Besides, it was Monday and that was Fiddlers' Night at Kelly's. The music would stir our souls and prepare us for the good fight!

At the pub, we ordered our favorite, vegetarian chili and cornbread. We decided against drinks because we feared the meeting would run long, and we needed to keep our wits about us, so we were surprised when our waitress, Sally, returned with two cold beers.

Anna politely said, "I'm sorry, but we didn't order these."

Sally glanced over her shoulder and responded with a wink, "I know, but he did."

Three freshly shaven men nodded at us from the back of the pub, but only the youngest smiled. Anna and I recognized him instantly. It was Jake. We smiled back and told Sally to tell the gentleman thank you.

"Is he trying to fill us with alcohol so we slur our words and appear like fools in front of the whole town?" I asked Anna in a whisper.

"I'm sure that's not his plan, but I do think he wants our attention."

"You mean he wants *your* attention. I'm fairly certain he's not interested in me. Besides, I'm taken."

"Very funny, Mom," Anna said, raising an eyebrow.

"Well, don't look now, but he's headed our way."

In a second, Jake was standing by our table, looking down at us with those piercing blue eyes. I could almost hear Anna's heart beating as Jake greeted us.

"Hi. I almost didn't recognize you in this festive setting. An Irish pub is so different from a cemetery, but now that I see the two of you together, side by side, I can see the resemblance. You look like sisters."

"You're cute, but not that cute," I said in my best teacher's voice. "This is my daughter, Anna. I believe you met this morning on Beacon Hill."

"Yes, I remember," said Jake as he turned bright red. He took a moment to find his voice again and carefully continued. "I'm guessing you're going to the meeting tonight."

"Yes, we'll be headed over there as soon as we finish dinner," said Anna as Sally set two steaming bowls of chili down on our table.

"I'll probably see you there. Enjoy the chili. I've got a feeling it's going to be a spicy night!" Jake flashed his charming smile and turned to leave, but he wasn't fast enough to escape without hearing my parting shot.

"I hope you had the chili, too, because you're going to have to breathe fire to win tonight!"

Anna leaned back, crossed her arms, and glared at me. In stony silence, she mouthed the words, *How could you?* And then she ran to catch Jake at the door. She even left her smart phone on the table. While she grabbed the closing door with her left hand, she touched his shoulder with her right, and called out, "Jake!"

Jake turned. When he saw Anna's face only inches from his own, he blinked in surprise and said nothing. Anna spoke. I couldn't hear what she said, but I could see Jake's reaction. He was nodding.

* * *

"Don't worry," said Jake with a forgiving smile. "Your mom is just trying to protect the city she loves. I admire her passion, but maybe you and I should exchange cell numbers so we can communicate in a less confrontational way. You know, text like friends."

Anna laughed. "That's a great idea!" She patted her pockets in search of her phone, glanced back at the table, and sighed. "But I left my phone on the table where my mother is sitting. Gosh, this is awkward."

Without missing a beat, Jake produced a pen from his pocket and said, "Let me see your hand."

Anna held up her hand, and Jake quickly wrote his seven digits. "Now you can call me."

Looking at her palm, Anna asked, "Don't you have a business card?"

"Yes, but this isn't business; it's personal! Besides, I've always wanted to write my number on the palm of a pretty girl's hand. They do it in the movies, right?"

Anna stepped back and smiled. "You're a complicated guy, Jake, and I'll probably call you because I'm curious."

Then she let him go, but she didn't move until he looked back and waved. He was standing on the corner under the glow of the streetlight, and he was smiling, too.

CHAPTER 7

2013

When Anna and I arrived at City Hall, most of the seats were already taken, but Doris was sitting up front, and she had saved us a couple. As I sat down, I told her about running into Jake at the pub.

Doris nodded in his direction and quietly said, "He walked in about fifteen minutes ago with Bath's attorney and another man in an expensive suit who is probably representing the DOT. All three of them looked serious. The two gentlemen carrying legal pads looked like they were ready to kill a moose."

"They look perfectly harmless to me," Anna chided.

"Well, Anna, you are not completely impartial when it comes to Captain America over there," I volleyed back with a wink at Doris.

At six o'clock sharp, the councilmen entered the hall and sat down at a long mahogany table in front of the crowd. The chair of the City Council, Bill Marston, pounded his gavel to call the meeting to order. He seemed on edge, and his clenched jaw suggested that this was not business as usual. For a moment, I felt like I was in a courtroom and the judge was about to pass a brutal sentence. I guess Jake and I were both right. It was going to be a stressful evening.

"Ladies and gentlemen, your attention, please!" As a former litigator, Bill Marston was adept at bringing a room to order. He waited for complete silence, took a long sip of water, and then spoke in a loud, clear voice.

"It has come to the City Council's attention that many of you are against the Maine DOT's plan to widen Beacon Street because it will destroy the oldest section of the Beacon Hill Cemetery. Despite the fact that we approved the Old Route 1 Improvement Project several months ago, we will review the details tonight in order to satisfy those who feel that the residents were not adequately informed about the specifics of the plan and that the council's decision does not represent their wishes. Be advised that the City Council has the authority to resolve this issue in compliance with Maine law, and with our approval, the DOT has the right to move forward on this project. However, we are willing to entertain suggestions at this time to improve the plan. Let's keep our discussion civil and productive. The director of Nequasset Preservation, Incorporated, Doris Van der Waag, will speak first. Mrs. Van der Waag, the floor is yours."

Doris stood up and turned to address the standing-room-only crowd. The news of tonight's meeting had spread fast, and the large turnout showed that Doris and I were not the only history buffs in Maine's City of Ships. As a community, Bath has the lively heart of an artist but the serious soul of a historian. Sitting in the middle of City Hall, I was surrounded by painters, singers, songwriters, architects, teachers, carpenters, lawyers, entrepreneurs, engineers, poets, gardeners, and doctors. At the end of the day, they were all historians. In fact, one of the greatest fundraisers ever created by the Main Street Bath Association is a game night called "So You Think You Know

Bath?" Every year on a cold night in March, four or five community groups each field a team to prove that they know Bath's maritime history best. The NPI team was the reigning champion, and Doris Van der Waag was the captain of the team.

"Thank you, Mr. Marston, and members of the City Council, for giving me this opportunity to speak out against Maine DOT's plan to widen Beacon Street. Clearly, there has been a terrible mistake because the project calls for the demolition of Section One of the Beacon Hill Cemetery, and we haven't discussed what should be done with the remains of the souls buried in that section. I believe I speak for the majority of Bath residents when I say that Bath is committed to *preserving* history, not destroying it. Our city is a maritime treasure, and we cannot quietly stand by and allow the state to exhume the graves of the founding families of Bath for the sole purpose of alleviating traffic on Route 1. We are talking about the graves of shipbuilding giants and legendary sea captains. There are also heroes of the Revolutionary War, the War of 1812, and the Civil War buried on that hill. How can we exhume their graves without a just measure of dignity? Is this the way we honor those who sacrificed their lives in order to create one of the greatest shipbuilding cities in the world?" Doris's voice climbed with emotion, and then it came down again to end softly and dramatically.

"My dear friends," she concluded, "I think we need a better plan."

When Doris sat down, the crowd erupted in applause and called for a vote. Bill Marston had to use his gavel again to restore order.

"Ladies and gentleman, for the sake of civility and peace, let's quiet down and allow the DOT's representative a chance to respond. Mr. Summers, it's your turn."

Jake stood up, and I could see that his neck was flaming red, but his face appeared calm and his words sounded clear and steady as he began to address the assembly.

"I think everyone in this hall knows the chokehold Route 1 poses for the mid-coast of Maine. Let's be honest: some realtors advise against buying property north of the Sagadahoc Bridge because it will take forever to get to it during the high season from the first of April to the thirty-first of October. Local and state officials have been aware of the problem for years, and engineers have spent countless hours studying the problem and developing possible solutions. I'm here to tell you that we can solve the problem if you will let us. When we open up Old Route 1 as an alternate to US Route 1, there will be a surge of economic growth, long overdue, in Sagadahoc and Lincoln Counties. Before we build a second bridge, however, we have to begin to widen the old route, and that includes Beacon Street. Maine DOT is ready to implement the best possible plan. Furthermore, our research shows that the family gravesites in Section One have not been added to or even visited by family members in over seventy-five years. According to state law, if a cemetery plot owned by a family has not been used in seventy-five years, the plot of land can be resold. Realistically speaking, those plots have not been used in over two hundred years…"

Suddenly, I felt my body stand up as if the action was completely involuntary, and I heard my voice interrupt Jake's argument.

"Wait a minute, Mr. Summers," I said in a quivering voice. "Many of those tombstones promise perpetual care."

"Mrs. Malone, with all due respect, in legal terms, 'perpetual care' simply means the cemetery has to be mowed. Many of the tombstones on Beacon Hill are broken, and the inscriptions are difficult, if not impossible, to read because of time, weather, and, in some sad cases, vandalism. I'm sorry, but the truth is, few if any family members remain in the same community over a period of one hundred years or more."

In a steadier voice, I said, "You seem to have all the answers, but you're overlooking Bath's commitment to preserve its history. Perhaps there are no living relatives in the area to place flowers at those graves, but members of this community recognize those family names. The councilman who just called this meeting to order, Bill Marston, bears a name that repeats and repeats throughout the history of Bath. Now, I don't know if Bill Marston puts flowers on any or all of the Marston graves, but I'm sure he recognizes their contribution to our City of Ships. Maybe you should ask him!"

"Mrs. Malone, let's not get personal. I'm not expressing feelings; I'm just stating facts. I'm an engineer, and I'm trying to do my job," said Jake, looking straight ahead with his shoulders thrown back like a sentry at his post. No one had to view his service record to know that he was a veteran. His posture and overall body language validated his military service.

I had run out of words, and, truth be told, I was feeling rather embarrassed, so I abruptly sat down and looked at the floor. I didn't dare look at Anna because I knew she would be furious with me for attacking Jake in front of a large crowd of people. Clearly, she liked this tall, handsome Captain America who I had just tried to publicly insult, though in a twist of fate, I was the one who was whipped, not Jake. Anna must have felt my pain because she reached over and tapped my knee in a loving way.

"It's okay, Mom. Everyone knows that your heart is in the right place, and you just want to preserve Bath's important history."

I nodded and whispered, "Thank you, honey," then sat quietly for at least another hour while other citizens spoke out against the DOT's plan. Finally, Bill Marston pounded his gavel and adjourned the meeting with a promise on behalf of the City Council to consider all the views expressed that night before issuing the city's final decision.

It was a relief to step out into the cool night air. The moon over Bath was full and bright that night, and it helped to lift my spirit as well as my eyes. After gazing up at the moon and the stars, I looked out to Front Street just in time to see Jake's pickup truck pull out of a nearby parking spot and tear down the street. As I wondered why young men used cars and trucks to express their emotions, I noticed an Iraq decal on the rear bumper of his truck, and my thoughts collided with reality. That word, *Iraq*, a singular noun and a faraway country, suggested a life interrupted. When Ty and I used to take the kids on long road trips, we often saw bumper stickers that encouraged us to travel to entertaining destinations like Hilton Head, Cape Cod, and my personal favorite, Popham Beach. The bumper sticker on Jake's truck carried a different message. Most American families would not consider Iraq as a vacation destination.

On the walk home, I told Anna how badly I felt about having to oppose Jake's work, and she seemed to genuinely understand.

"It's a tough situation. You know what they say in baseball."

"No, Anna, I don't know. What do they say in baseball?"

"You can't steal second with your foot on first."

"Okay, now I'm really lost," I sighed.

"Sometimes you have to take a risk in order to win, and we can't move forward unless we're willing to accept change. I bet Jake doesn't like to think about the past because it's too painful. If you're lucky enough to survive a war, you probably don't want to look back. And you probably try to avoid cemeteries."

"Why Anna, I believe your NYU education is paying dividends. If you're right, Jake is approaching this from a very different perspective than NPI. I'm afraid our 'Save the Cemetery Campaign' has encountered a fire-breathing dragon, and we're directly in its line of fire!"

I looked out across the water and wondered how long it would take to build a new road and perhaps another bridge across the Kennebec. Like every member of NPI, I believed Long Reach to be a national treasure, but I also realized that change is inevitable, and great water views are coveted by developers yearning to make money. If it were possible to save time in a bottle, NPI would champion that cause, and Doris and I would gladly fill hundreds of bottles. We might not be able to stop all the bulldozers in Bath, but today we had saved some sacred ground, at least for a little while. When I turned to tell Anna how I felt about our small victory, I realized she was no longer thinking about improving roads or saving cemeteries. The sky was filled with stars, and Anna was studying them as if she were about to reach for one. I wondered if Jake's mere presence might give her a reason to fly again.

Shortly after we arrived home, I watched Anna climb the gently curving staircase at the front of our house. Her left hand glided over the bannister, while her right hand sent a text message. There wasn't a doubt in my mind that the message was for Jake. His phone number was written in blue on the palm of her hand.

CHAPTER 8

2013

As Anna hurried along the dock to the Blue Heron, her long, curly hair danced in the wind. She used her fingers to brush it back and checked her watch. It was 12:15. She was late. A party of four was leaving when she rushed through the open door. The hostess greeted her with a menu.

How many in your party?"

"I'm meeting someone."

"Oh, I believe he's waiting for you." She glanced over at the corner table, and asked, "Is that him?"

"Yes."

"Well, follow me," she said in a high, perky voice.

When Jake looked up, he wanted to whistle, but he checked that impulse and smiled instead.

"I was beginning to think you weren't coming."

"Are you kidding? I would never miss an opportunity to have lunch at Robinhood Cove. Look at that view!"

Jake grinned like a schoolboy. "I'd say the view I'm enjoying right now is amazing." And then he turned to look out the window. "And the water view is pretty, too."

Anna sat down, looked directly at Jake, and said, "You know, you're a shameless flirt. I'm serious. I love this cove. It has a soothing effect on me."

Jake returned Anna's gaze and playfully said, "It has the opposite effect on me."

"What do you mean?"

As he pretended to read the menu, Jake answered, "Beauty excites me."

Anna let those three little words hang in the air like Cupid's arrow. She looked at her menu and said, "We should order. I'm famished."

By the time the fish and chips arrived, Anna and Jake were chatting up a storm. They were both good storytellers, and they both had a good sense of humor. Anna talked about growing up with two brothers, and Jake talked about growing up as an only child. Because his mother had died in a skiing accident when he was barely three years old, he felt as if he had grown up in his dad's auto repair shop. And Anna's eyes opened a little wider when he told her he could fix cars before he could drive them.

When the waitress returned and asked if they wanted to order dessert, Anna shook her head, but Jake said, "I'll have the blueberry cobbler with vanilla ice cream on top. And could you bring an extra spoon for my friend here?"

Anna laughed. "So we're friends now?"

Jake wrapped his hand around his glass of hard cider and nodded. "It seems to be going well!" He took a sip before making a serious confession. "You know, I looked you up online."

"I'm not surprised. My mom looked you up."

Jake shook his head.

"Your mom is quite a force. Did she uncover anything interesting?"

"She found your service record…and it's impressive."

Jake took another swallow of his hard cider.

"Let's not talk about Iraq. Today is a good day. I don't want to do a rain dance."

Anna agreed, but she wasn't ready to stop talking.

"Okay, but I'm curious. What did you find out about me?"

Jake's grin was back. "Congratulations! You've managed to keep a low profile, but I did find an article that NYU published online about you. It talked about a film you were producing in Seattle…"

"*Coffee Wars.*"

"Yes, that's the one, and I've seen it. It was a good movie. As soon as I left the theater, I had to find a Northwest Coffee House and order a latte."

The door was open. Anna could tell Jake what had broken her heart and almost extinguished her voice as a writer. She waited as the server placed a decadent dessert on the table.

"I was only an associate producer on that film," said Anna as she carefully folded her napkin and struggled to find the right words. "I wrote most of the screenplay, but I didn't receive a single writing credit."

Jake was quiet. He looked out the window and saw an osprey take flight.

Anna looked up teary-eyed. "I've always been a writer. My dream was to become a screenwriter. That didn't happen."

"Not yet," said Jake quietly. "You were right about this place. It's easy to find peace here. But I was right, too. This little cove on the Sasanoa River is exciting because it inspires beauty. And I believe it will inspire you."

Anna took a deep breath. "For an engineer, you have a way with words."

* * *

I was working in the garden when Anna pulled into the driveway. My constant companion, Freckles, barked and ran to greet her. Of course, I followed.

"How did it go?" I asked.

"How did what go?"

"How was your lunch date with Jake?"

Anna gave me her stop-right-there look. "It wasn't a date. I'm not dating anyone."

"Okay, how was the Blue Heron?"

"It was wonderful as usual."

As I took off my gardening gloves, I shook my head and wondered out loud. "Blue must be Maine's favorite color. Have you ever noticed how all the best places have *blue* in their names?"

"Yes, his eyes are amazing. I think they're ocean blue."

I dropped my glove, but I didn't look down.

"Oh, honey, you may not be dating, but you've definitely met someone."

I think my observation caught Anna by surprise because she didn't say another word. She opened the side door and entered the house. I wanted to give her space, so I walked back to the garden with Freckles right behind me.

CHAPTER 9

1875

Thomas was sitting on the thin mattress of his monk-like bed in the dormitory of Bowdoin College, and his father was sitting on his roommate's bed. The two men faced each other, but neither one was talking. Heavy silence hung between them until Daniel McGowan, Thomas's roommate and friend, entered the room.

"Good afternoon, Captain Goss," said Daniel in the most respectful voice he could muster. This was clearly an unexpected visit because Thomas was still in the clothes he had worn yesterday, and he looked like hell. Daniel suspected that his friend had slept in those clothes, but he hadn't slept in their room, so who knew what time he might have returned to their dormitory? It wasn't before eight a.m. when they were both supposed to be in their philosophy class.

"Hello, Daniel," said Henry. "Good to see you again. How is your father doing? We miss him at the shipyard."

Daniel was about to answer when Thomas interjected, "Can you excuse us for a minute? My father and I are in the middle of a conversation."

"Of course!" said Daniel, a bit surprised because he hadn't heard either of them say a word to each other. As he turned to leave the room, he looked directly at Henry and said, "It's good to see you, too, Captain Goss. I'll tell my father you asked about him. That will please him."

"Thomas, that was rude," Henry said after Daniel had left the room.

"No, Father, that was necessary. We really have to talk. I hate being cooped up in this stuffy old college with these arrogant rich boys."

"Daniel McGowan is hardly an arrogant rich boy. Bowdoin is one of the finest schools in the country, and the best college in Maine."

"I know all of that, and it's your alma mater, but it is not right for me. I would rather be at sea on a ship sailing to foreign ports and seeing the world. I'm twenty years old and still less than twenty miles from home. I feel as if all of these tall pines are closing in on me, and I can't breathe."

"I don't think it's the trees that affect your breathing. You drink and gamble with your rowing mates every night of the week. Your coach tells me you've missed five practices, but you're still the strongest man in the boat. Your teachers tell me you're bright, but you rarely attend class. Thomas, why are you trying to destroy your future?"

Thomas looked straight into his father's eyes and said, "Maybe I don't deserve a future." And silence filled the room again.

Seconds passed, but they seemed more like minutes, and when Henry responded, his voice was low and gentle. "You deserve a brilliant future, Thomas. You are the sun and the moon and the stars in your mother's eyes and in my eyes, too."

"That is because I'm the only one who survived. I should be following in my brothers' footsteps. They never even had a chance to grow up. Jonathan would have been taller than me. He would have been a better rower. He would have sat in the middle of the boat. I'm the stroke.

And Francis, he was the smart one. He would have been valedictorian of his class and gone on to medical school at Harvard. Face it, Father, I was the runt of the litter, and I only succeed at disappointing both you and Mother."

"Nonsense!" Henry said with anger and sadness in equal measure. "You were just six when your brothers died. And you don't know who would have been the tallest or smartest. But by sending you to Riggsville, your mother saved your life. And I believe you were saved for a purpose."

"I wish I had died with Jonathan and Francis. I belonged with them," Thomas said quietly.

"No, Thomas. You belonged with us, your mother and me. I fear we would have lost our purpose for living if you had not survived."

In thought, Henry returned to that dire time. He remembered that it took months to reach Bath after receiving word of his sons' fatal illness. Captain McGowan's ship, the *Ellie*, was struck with heavy gales. Several crewmen, including the cook, were washed overboard and lost. Henry was terrified that he would never reach home. But Trufant's mighty brig survived the storm, and so did he and his dear friend, Robert McGowan. Unfortunately, their loved ones at home did not fare as well. Two of Henry's three sons, his mother-in-law, and Robert's wife all died before they arrived. Henry recalled the sorrow that engulfed him when he returned to Bath, opened the front door to his once happy home, and felt its emptiness.

Henry became quiet and closed his eyes as if in prayer until Thomas's voice broke the silence.

"I never got to say goodbye to any of them, and I can't remember their faces."

Henry stood up and moved across the room to sit next to Thomas and put his arm around him, something he hadn't done in years. With his touch, Thomas began to cry and then sob uncontrollably, shaking the small dorm room with deep sorrow.

Henry rubbed his son's shoulder as he gently whispered, "Jonathan said something to your mother before he died that we should have shared with you a long time ago. He told her that you would be the one to go to sea, and you would become the best sea captain in our family's fleet. Your brother, as young as he was, imagined that you would be the mariner that he and Francis would never be, and he wanted you to know that your brothers would always be standing with you looking toward the horizon."

Thomas used the long sleeve of his cotton shirt to wipe the tears from his face, and, like a small child, rested his head for a brief moment on Henry's chest before he stood up to face him.

"If all that is true, then I know what I have to do," said Thomas. "I have to leave these safe, ivy-covered buildings and go to sea to test my courage and see the world."

Henry stood and looked into his son's eyes. "Son, listen to me. If you finish this semester, you will have completed two years at Bowdoin, and I will be able to secure you a first-mate slot on a ship in the Gannett fleet. Perhaps one of their captains would agree to sign you on for a voyage. What do you say?"

"All right, Father. I will stay for this semester, but only this one."

"June will be here before you know it," said Henry with his heavy coat draped over his left arm and his right hand on the doorknob. He looked back at Thomas and added, "I love you, Son." Then he turned and left before Thomas could respond.

* * *

The next day, Henry made a point of walking over to the Gannett Shipyard. Arthur Gannett was one of the richest and most influential men in Bath. His shipbuilding business had suffered during the war, but he and his brother, William, had managed to keep their yard open. Now, with a renewed demand for merchant ships, the

Gannett family was hoping to expand their shipyard along Long Reach. As members of one of the founding families of Bath, all of the men in the Gannett family were involved in shipping. If they weren't building ships, they were selling them or sailing them or negotiating contracts for their cargo. In some maritime circles, the Gannetts were known as American royalty. Henry Goss knew most of them as neighbors. In 1866, when Henry and his partner had bought Johnson Rideout's old shipyard, directly north of the Gannett Shipyard, Arthur was not pleased about the new competition in the neighborhood, but he realized that Henry had become a master builder despite great personal loss and had earned his respect.

Henry entered the Gannett shipping office on Front Street at three o'clock, which was a good time to catch Arthur at his desk. When the door slammed shut, Arthur looked up from his ledger and quickly offered him a seat.

"Hello, Henry. Come in and sit down. I haven't seen you in weeks. The Goss and Sawyer Shipbuilding Company must be busy!"

Henry sat in the big armchair next to Arthur's massive desk and laughed. "Yes, all the Bath shipyards have been busy. No one is complaining on the docks this year. In fact, I read a report yesterday that the tonnage presently owned by Bath is exceeded only by New York, Philadelphia, Boston, and San Francisco. Profits are up, unemployment is down, and the only shortage in Bath is a room for rent!"

"You've done well, Henry, considering that you and Ethan purchased the Rideout yard less than ten years ago. The level of activity along Long Reach now reminds me of our glory days before the war. And your firm deserves much of the credit for Bath's comeback. Your yard is one of the largest in the city, and some say that at your rate of productivity, you may well become the largest shipbuilding plant in the United States. Why, the Philadelphia press is praising you for your newest ship, the *City of*

Philadelphia! Some government inspectors believe it's the finest ship they have ever seen!"

"I'm sure those inspectors are native Philadelphians who are simply smitten by the ship's grand name," Henry replied humbly.

"I'm not so sure of that," Arthur responded. "Your mechanics are the finest in the city, and you are using the best materials. What was that five-hundred-ton schooner you built in '71?"

"Are you referring to the *Calvin P. Harris*?"

"Yes, that's the one. You received high marks for that beauty, and you deserved the praise. You built that schooner with all of the latest improvements. Goss and Sawyer is one of the most progressive firms in the country!"

"Thank you, Arthur. Your kind words humble me, and your company's enduring success, despite the horror and destruction of the war, continues to inspire all of the shipbuilders in America."

"Well, I think all of this good news deserves a toast, don't you?" asked Arthur as he reached for the brandy and two shot glasses on the small table near his desk. "And I must ask, is this solely a social visit?"

Henry took a moment to sample the brandy and then another moment to clear his throat. "No, it is not entirely social. I do have a favor to ask. My son, Thomas, will be leaving Bowdoin in June after he completes his second year of study. He would like to go to sea as a first mate, and I was wondering if your fleet would have an opportunity for him."

"Has he been to sea before?"

"He and his mother accompanied me on my last voyage in 1862, when I took command of the *Ellie* to relieve Captain Robert McGowan. Thomas was quite young, but he adapted quickly to life at sea and seemed to enjoy the almost eighteen months he spent aboard ship."

"I remember how consumption swept through the city at the beginning of the war. It was as if we were fighting on two fronts. One front was south of the Mason-Dixon line, and the other was here at home. You lost two little boys and your mother-in-law, Hannah Riggs. Am I right?"

"Yes," said Henry. "Captain McGowan brought me the news and offered me a swift passage home. At the time, he didn't know his wife was also stricken. Johnson Rideout's son, Nathan, was my first mate, and he took command of my ship when I departed."

Arthur concluded in a somber voice. "And neither he nor the *Roanoke* were ever seen again. The *Roanoke* was officially reported missing two years later."

"The winds of fate have clearly carried us all to our intended destinations. If Nathan Rideout had lived, he probably would have taken over his father's shipyard, and I would not be a master shipbuilder today."

Arthur leaned back in his chair and said, "Like you, Henry, I believe in fate. Now tell me, what happened to Captain McGowan?"

"After his wife died of consumption, he retired from the sea to take care of his young son."

Henry was quiet for a moment as he remembered the series of events that had affected his life so dramatically. If Robert had not retired, he might never have commanded the *Ellie* nor had the inclination to take his wife and Thomas on a voyage around Cape Horn to Hong Kong and back again. He believed that voyage had saved his wife's sanity and imbued his only surviving son with an everlasting love for the sea.

Arthur poked Henry's memory with a simple question. "He remarried, didn't he?"

"Yes. A few years after Clare's death, he met Catherine O'Day, and they were married within a year. They have a little girl named Mary Rose, and they're enjoying a good life on a farm in Bowdoinham. His son, Daniel, is now a second-year student at Bowdoin College, and remains my son's good friend."

Arthur thought for a moment and said, "Captain

Sam Gannett is my brother William's son, and he is in command of *El Capitan*. I believe he is looking for a new mate. *El Capitan* will be departing New York for San Francisco in June, and I will request that Sam take your son aboard. Considering his Bowdoin education, and the fact that he sailed around Cape Horn at an early age, I trust he will serve the Gannett fleet well."

CHAPTER 10

1875

Honoring a gentleman's agreement, Henry arrived at Grand Central Station with his wife and son on June 21, 1875. The next day Thomas Goss stood on the dock at South Street in New York's busy harbor. His heavy brown duffel bag stood beside him while he hugged his mother goodbye. At fifty-two years of age, Charlotte was thinner than she had once been, and there were lots of fine lines beneath her eyes, but she was still a luminous beauty, and her lilting, soft voice sounded exactly the same. As Thomas breathed in her sweet scent, he realized that while he was at sea he would not miss the earth beneath his feet as much as he would miss his mother's loving embrace. He would also miss her encouragement. She had a gift for saying what you needed to hear at exactly the right moment, and she was the only person he had ever fully trusted with his innermost thoughts. Surrounded by scores of salty sailors on the dock, he knew he would feel alone aboard ship, and that reality was daunting.

"I'm going to make you proud," he whispered in her ear.

And she whispered back, "You already have, my darling boy."

Henry cleared his throat and stepped a little closer to his wife and son.

Thomas turned toward his father and reached out his hand, but Henry batted it away so that he could give his son a hug. Clearly, Arthur Gannett's assessment of Henry had been correct. He was indeed a progressive thinker. Since losing two sons, Henry believed it was important to express emotions, especially love. In fact, he often told his friends, and even his crews at the shipyard, that they should tell the people dearest to them how they felt because tomorrow was promised to no one.

"Father, I won't disappoint you," said Thomas as he threw his duffel onto his left shoulder.

"I have confidence in you. Be brave, Thomas, and remain strong. Your mother and I love you."

Thomas swallowed hard as he turned away from his parents and stepped toward the ship. "I love you, too," he said, without looking back. His mother and father could not see the emotion on his face as he refused to cry and willed his tears away. He was about to board *El Capitan*. School days were over.

Once on board, Thomas headed to the forecastle and found his quarters, a tiny cubicle with a hammock, a trunk, and a canvas door to afford a semblance of privacy. He quickly unpacked his bag, placing his clothes and personal items in the trunk. When the only item remaining at the bottom of his duffel was a bottle of rum, Thomas paused. He decided to leave it there, placed the sturdy bag under his hammock, and proceeded aft to the quarterdeck. Bathed in bright June sunlight, the blue water of the Atlantic sparkled, and Thomas's heartbeat quickened. He looked up to see Captain Sam Gannett standing with two young women at the top of the short stairway leading to the captain's cabin. Although he was not surprised to see the captain, he was stunned to see the ladies and stumbled as he tried to introduce himself.

"Good morning, Captain; good morning, ladies," said Thomas, bowing slightly. "Allow me to introduce myself. I'm Thomas Goss, your new first mate. It's good to be aboard."

For a moment, Captain Gannett looked hard at Thomas, but then offered his hand and said, "Welcome, Thomas. I am a great admirer of your father's work. He is not only a respected ship master, but a renowned shipbuilder, as well. If you are half the man he is, *El Capitan* is lucky to have you."

"Thank you, Captain," said Thomas. "I will certainly try to be worthy of my family's name."

"I'm confident you will do just that," the captain said with a smile. "Now, let me introduce you to my two sisters, Miss Celia Gannett and Miss Sarah Gannett. They will be joining us on this voyage."

Celia, a few years older and slightly more reserved, nodded hello, but Sarah reached out to shake Thomas's hand. "Call me Sadie. Everyone does."

Sarah's sweet smile and dreamy blue eyes caught Thomas off guard. He had to clear his throat twice before he managed to say, "Good morning! I think you're too pretty to be called Sadie. It's a pleasure to meet you, Sarah."

Sam Gannett chuckled out loud as he observed Thomas's reaction to his little sister, and he wasn't the least bit surprised that Celia was overlooked.

* * *

On the long passage from New York Harbor to Montevideo, Uruguay, Thomas's days were filled with standing the port watch for four hours at a time and supervising the boatswain, who was in charge of scraping and painting the ship and repairing the rigging and sails. As first mate, Thomas also kept the log book, studied the weather, and helped the captain with navigation. There was no time for idleness, but he did have to eat, and a few weeks after hauling anchor in New York, Captain Gannett invited him to dine in his cabin along with Celia and Sarah. Thomas shaved and put on a clean shirt for the occasion. When he knocked at the cabin door, a steward opened it and directed him to his seat at a long mahogany table that was set with fine china, sterling silver, and crystal. After weeks at sea, it was a dazzling sight—but not as stunning as Celia and Sarah, who were already seated at the table. In the soft glow of six candles, set in two ornate candelabras, Celia's long chestnut hair and Sarah's golden locks made Thomas blink in disbelief. And then Captain Gannett's gruff voice interrupted his dream.

"Sit down, Thomas. You've been working hard, and you deserve a short respite. Besides, I fear my sisters are getting bored, and I was hoping you could distract them this evening. I hear you're quite a storyteller, and long voyages are tedious without a few tall tales."

Sarah looked intently at Thomas with a hint of lust in her eye, but Celia seemed embarrassed. She looked away and fiddled with her napkin. Thomas sat down, placed a white linen napkin, monogrammed with the captain's initials, *SEG*, on his lap, and prepared for a feast. According to the rumors aboard ship, the Chinese cook had been trained in the emperor's palace, and Thomas was yearning for meat and potatoes. When the steward set his plate in front of him, his salivary glands awakened. After his first bite of juicy pork tenderloin, he looked across the table at Sarah and thought that he had passed through the pearly gates of heaven. He chewed slowly and savored the perfectly prepared meat before reaching for the bread basket near his plate.

As he smeared a fresh biscuit with coveted butter, reserved only for officers, the steward poured more wine, and Celia seized the moment to admire his handsome face. She and her sister had been forced to remain in their cabins because of the strong gales and rough seas. They had kept their hands and minds occupied with music and needlework, but until now neither sister had enjoyed the voyage. By the time the steward served the rice pudding, it was crystal clear that the two Gannett sisters found Thomas beguiling. Celia, who had always been the more generous and caring sister, didn't even feel guilty about the luxurious dinner they had been served. In the pleasure of the moment, she forgot that the sailors on board were washing their dried food down with gallons of beer and putting grease on their hard biscuits while they enjoyed their sweet dessert.

After dinner, Captain Gannett offered Thomas a glass of whiskey and a Cuban cigar, and he poured two glasses of sherry for his sisters. Thomas started talking about rowing days at Bowdoin, and the thrill of stroking for the eight-man boat against Harvard in the fall of 1874. His deep baritone voice seemed to cast a net around Sarah's heart, and Celia's, too. They all laughed when he described some of the pranks he had pulled on his roommate and teammate, Daniel McGowan. It was hard to imagine a serious man like Thomas moving Daniel's bed and dresser into the hallway in the middle of the night, but Thomas convinced them it had happened.

When there was finally a long, quiet pause, Captain Gannett asked his sisters if they would like to add some music to the evening's entertainment, and Celia quickly moved toward the small upright piano against the cabin's wall. She sat down and let her hands dance across the keys. Together, Sarah and Celia began to sing "Shenandoah" in sweet, angelic voices. And for the first time since leaving home, Thomas did not feel lost or alone. He would sleep well that night and dream of pretty girls in fancy dresses, and in the morning he would remember the refrain of one of his favorite songs, and the words would repeat in his head for days to come.

O Shenandoah, I long to hear you.
Away, you rolling river.
O Shenandoah, I long to hear you.
Away, I'm bound away
'Cross the wide Missouri…

Unfortunately, all the evenings aboard ship were not as pleasurable as the night he had told stories in the captain's cabin and listened to the Gannett sisters sing. Off of Cape Horn, *El Capitan* was surprised by heavy weather early one morning. A sailor who had just taken in the top-gallant sails noticed a particularly dark-looking squall on the rise and alerted Thomas. For at least twenty minutes, the ship was punished with thrashing waves and violent gales. An able seaman, affectionately known as the Swede, was washed overboard, and three sailors were injured as they tried to get more sail off of the ship. The mainsail was torn, and all the staysails were split. When the fierce wind and rain finally ceased, every member of the crew was soaked through and completely exhausted. Thomas recorded the damages in the ship's log and noted the loss of a good sailor and the serious injury of the boatswain. Rounding the Cape was a victory, but it came at a high price. The crew was demoralized, and Thomas feared the remainder of the passage would be difficult.

* * *

A month later, off the coast of Peru, near the port of Callao, Thomas felt dizzy, but not because he was dreaming of the captain's two sisters. Now his head was hurting because he feared the captain's wrath.

"Captain, may I stop this cruel and unusual punishment? The second mate and I have been force-feeding this sailor for three days. If we continue, his digestive system will fail, and I can assure you he will die a slow and painful death."

"Are you questioning my judgment, Mr. Goss?"

"No, sir, I am not."

"Good! Now let me show you how we maintain discipline aboard ship."

The captain grabbed the belaying pin that Thomas had set down and proceeded to strike the prisoner's jaw. Then he handed the pin to Thomas and commanded, "Strike this man's jaw every time he stops eating!"

Thomas stepped back, fully expecting the captain to strike his face as well. "Sir, I am only alerting you to the fact that we will all be accused of murder if this sailor dies. His only crime is that he requested more food for the crew."

"My only mistake, Thomas, is that I thought you were ready to take command. If you are too weak to discipline the sailors aboard ship, they will take control. Open your eyes, man. This sailor is an instigator. There's one on every voyage. If it wasn't the food, he would have found another hardship to complain about. Disobedience cannot be tolerated!"

"Respectfully, I disagree, Captain. What the sailor said was true. Yesterday, Mr. Hague discovered a sailor stealing slush grease. That grease is intended for the masts and rigging, not biscuits. For the sailors, the quality and quantity of food aboard ship is substandard. We are sailing with insufficient provisions."

"You sound like a mama's boy! Carry out my orders, or it is you who will be force-fed until you can't swallow!"

With those stinging words, Captain Gannett grabbed the pin back from Thomas and swung it again at the sailor's swollen jaw. The broken sailor, still tied to a chair, spit up blood and vomited all over the captain's shoes.

Thomas raised his fists in anger. He was about to punch his captain when a voice in his head told him to stop. He turned and fled the cabin without saying another word and bolted down the stairs toward his own bunk. In his flight, he collided with Celia Gannett and knocked her down.

Even though Celia was literally taken off balance, she managed to apologize for getting in Thomas's way.

"I'm sorry," she said as she picked herself up and dusted off her skirt with her hands. "I should look where I'm going."

"No, it is I who should be sorry," said Thomas. "Please forgive me. Sometimes I'm a bull in a tea shop!"

"I doubt that's true. You're too agile to ever be clumsy, and you're too smart to ever be rude in a tea shop!"

For a moment, Thomas almost forgot where he was, and why he was there. In a weary voice, he said, "No one has ever called me too smart."

"You're being too humble. I was in your class at the Bath School. We started and finished eight grades together."

"Why don't I remember you? Did you have a nickname?" Thomas asked in disbelief.

"Yes, most of the class called me CC, the seal."

"Wait, I think I remember that nickname. I'm sorry. That was definitely unkind. I was a hellion back then, so I was probably one of those mean boys calling you names. Is there anything I can do to make amends?" said Thomas, beginning to relax and trying to forget the horror he had just witnessed.

"No, just call me Celia." She looked away, out toward the ocean, and tried to avoid Thomas's dark-brown eyes.

"That's easy enough," replied Thomas almost playfully.

Before Celia turned to walk away, she added, "And you could talk to me once in a while. Everyone could use a friend, even you. Don't take this the wrong way, but you looked awful a moment ago. You looked like someone who had just seen a ghost, or the devil himself."

Thomas stood speechless. Who was this sensitive creature with fawn-like eyes that he had just run over on the deck of the *El Capitan*? Could she see his fear? Did she know about her brother's cruelty? These unanswered questions kept Thomas from uttering a single word.

By the time he reached his quarters, his head was spinning again, and he dove into his hammock face first. A few minutes later, after his heart slowed down and he felt like he could think again, he sat up and reached under his hammock to retrieve the bottle of rum he had left in his duffel bag on his first day aboard ship. His hand shook a little as he poured the dark elixir down his throat. After a few long swallows, his thoughts began to slow until they eventually stopped altogether, and he fell into a deep sleep. He slept for hours, almost half a day, before he was awakened by the voice of the second mate, Ephraim Hague.

"Thomas, wake up!" Ephraim shouted as he shook his friend by the shoulders. "Captain Gannett has been looking for you. He wants to see you in his cabin right away."

With his eyes still closed, Thomas responded in a hoarse voice, "What time is it? How long have I been asleep?"

"I'm not sure," answered Ephraim. "Maybe eight hours."

"And the sailor—is he dead?" asked Thomas as he sat up and rubbed his eyes.

"The carpenter used all of the Epsom salts aboard ship to save him. His condition was dire for a while, but we think he'll survive. I swear that carpenter is as good as any doctor I've ever seen."

Thomas's head was aching, but he was relieved to hear that the grossly mistreated sailor was going to live. He tried to stand up but couldn't. Ephraim helped him to his feet.

"You'd better wash up before you report to the captain."

Later, when Thomas faced the captain for the first time since he had disobeyed his order to continue the sailor's punishment, he was clean-shaven and surprisingly calm. Ironically, the captain was calm as well.

"Thomas, I regret that you disagreed with my choice of punishment, but I attribute your gentle nature to your youth, and I trust you will develop a greater appreciation for a captain's need to maintain absolute control at sea. I see no reason to reprimand you further, but I advise you to toughen up quickly if you hope to command a ship of your own someday."

"Yes, sir!" said Thomas with a confident voice. "I do hope to be in command someday, and I will heed your advice. Thank you, Captain, for giving me the benefit of the doubt. In the future, I will obey orders without question."

Captain Gannett leaned back in his big chair and looked at the young man standing in front of him. "Well, then," he said, "if I have your word that you will obey orders and carry out your duties faithfully, I will send the letter of recommendation that I had prepared before this incident to our office in Bath."

Feeling relieved, and even a little exonerated, Thomas remained standing at attention as the captain continued.

"You should know that I have written my uncle Arthur, and I have emphasized your strengths. For example, you are the best predictor of weather I have ever known, and you are also one of the best navigators I've had under my command. As far as adding up latitude and longitude to pinpoint our location, you are figure perfect! In other words, with you on board we are exactly where we should be; therefore, I have recommended you be given your own command sooner rather than later."

"Thank you, Captain," said Thomas respectfully. "I am in your debt."

"You are welcome. Now get back to work—and don't make me regret what I have set in motion."

"Aye, aye, sir," said Thomas sharply, but as he closed the cabin door, he was struck by the sobering fact that he was now indebted to a man capable of unimaginable cruelty.

CHAPTER 11

2013

When I was teaching, I looked forward to the day off on Columbus Day because it was a holiday with few, if any, commitments, and I could enjoy a long run, a steamy shower, and a tall stack of pancakes. In keeping with that tradition, I woke up early and decided to take a long walk through Bath and along the river. It was a clear day, so I could admire Paul Revere's bell on the top of City Hall and the giant cranes towering over Bath Iron Works. I stopped at the edge of the Kennebec to drink in the orange hues of the tree line that stretched from Days Ferry to Arrowsic, and I let October fill me with hope.

As I turned toward home, I was feeling especially blessed because Anna had chosen to stay in Bath until she figured out her next move. Ty and I secretly missed the commotion of a house filled with children. Anna, Joe, and Frank had kept us incredibly entertained when they were little, and sometimes we wanted to turn the clock back to those wonder years. But since we couldn't, it was great to have our daughter home again, if only for a gap year. As I continued on my walk, I thought of something my mother used to say: "Life can change in a blink." I wondered what Stella Rose Donovan would have to say about the whirlwind of change affecting her granddaughter. Anna's career on the West Coast had just started to pick up speed when it suddenly stopped. Shortly after *Coffee Wars* premiered, she packed her bags and returned home. Ty and I were stunned. All of the reviews had been positive. The film was expected to be a hit at the box office, and it was. My intuition told me that Anna's decision to abandon her dreams had more to do with one man than an entire industry. We would hear the whole story when Anna was ready. For now, we had to be patient.

As I kept walking, my worries began to fade. I knew that Anna would recover; the wheels on her bus would turn, and her career would move forward again. I truly believed that Bath had caught Anna's heart in its silvery net. There was a new glow around my daughter's face, and I was hoping that Jake Summers would keep it there. When I finally arrived home, I found Anna standing on the side porch. She was about to leave.

"What took you so long, Mom? I just left you a note on the kitchen table explaining why I couldn't wait one more minute. I am desperate for a cup of Nick's freshly brewed coffee!"

"Sorry, honey. On a beautiful morning like this, I lose track of time."

Anna looked up at the sky, shook her head, and laughed before stepping back inside the house.

"I had a feeling you would be up and moving, so I thought I should seize the day, too. I thought we could walk downtown together and request the corner booth at the Blue Scone."

"Love must be in the air, Anna," I said with a wink. "You're so perky this morning! Give me a minute to jump in and out of the shower, and I'll be ready. Did you sleep well last night?"

"I actually didn't sleep well at all. In fact, I woke up at three o'clock in the morning to find uninvited guests in my cozy, back bedroom."

I raised an eyebrow. "What?"

"You heard me. In the wee hours of the morning, I had—"

"Okay, you're scaring me. Are you trying to tell me that our house is haunted? You know I don't believe in that sort of nonsense."

"I don't believe in it either, but last night was quite unusual. I woke up because I heard voices coming from the hallway. Didn't Doris tell us that there was probably a birthing room where the hallway and the master bath are now?"

"Yes, but that's not unusual for a house as old as ours. No one has implied that ghosts like to dwell in former birthing rooms."

Anna was fearless by nature, but she seemed genuinely unnerved by her uninvited guests, and that was alarming. "Were these spirits haunting you or the house?" I asked cautiously.

"I don't know, but I think an old birthing room would be a reasonable hangout for wandering spirits."

"Honey, I'm not ready to call in the ghost-busters just yet. Even you thought Doris was crazy for calling that shaman when she felt a ghostly presence in her house. Why don't you tell me about your dream? Maybe we can shed some light on this mystery together."

"Okay, two female spirits passed through my room's closed door. One appeared to be blond and the other brunette. They resembled each other, but they clearly had different personalities. Both were tall and slender, but only the brunette smiled. At first, the blonde seemed agitated, but the brunette started humming, and then she whispered something, and they started to sing in harmony. They were twirling around, and I could see that they were both wearing long dresses with stunning décolletage. Their high fashion suggested they were women of means in the late 1800s."

"The ghosts you're describing don't sound threatening at all. Who could they be, and why would they be visiting you?"

"I have no idea. But as soon as they stopped singing, they started to laugh, and that's when I fell back into a deep sleep. I slept soundly until an hour ago, and when I woke up, I was thinking of a girl's name, Cecilia, and I had a strong feeling that I would give that name to a baby girl someday."

"Isn't Cecilia the patron saint of musicians?"

"Only you would make that connection, Mom. Seriously, I just told you an unbelievable ghost story, and you're trying to make it a holy experience!"

I shook my head and laughed nervously.

"Oh, honey, it's not unusual for young women to dream about beautiful clothes, or the possibility of having a baby, and most women love to play the name game. I drove your dad crazy doing that. I think I was naming our children before he even proposed."

"This is different. I'm not planning a family right now. Heck, I'm not even in a serious relationship!"

"That may be true, but we can all dream, so don't mention this ghost story to Jake Summers. There's potential there."

Anna shook her head. "Mom, don't let your imagination run away with you!"

"Aha! We've established you're interested! Now I'm going to take a quick shower, and then we can walk downtown and let some highly caffeinated coffee stimulate our imaginations even more!"

A few minutes later, Anna and I were heading toward the library. We decided to cut through the park so we could savor the view of downtown Bath from the top of the "Rocky" steps. From that lofty corner, Anna and I could see the Kennebec River, the Sagadahoc Bridge, and a long row of quaint shops in beautiful red-brick buildings dating back to the nineteenth century. In the distance, the mighty cranes of Bath Iron Works seemed to be watching over it all. As we paused to breathe in the salty air, the Bath trolley came rumbling down the street, and Pete, the driver, rang its bell to say hello. We laughed and waved back. It felt good to be recognized. Anna appreciated the welcome, too. She started to talk candidly.

"I've been working on a screenplay. Maybe I'm feeling the magic of Bath because it's going well."

"Hmm…are you ready to share any details?"

Anna took a hair tie from her wrist and quickly pulled her hair back in a ponytail as if she were about to start a workout. Typically, she didn't talk about her writing projects until they were near completion.

"It's about a young Native American woman who teaches history at Tacoma High School. She grew up on a reservation, and she's from a long line of medicine women."

I shook my head. "How did you ever come up with that idea?"

"You know how much I love libraries. Well, when I was working on *Coffee Wars*, I visited the Tacoma library, and they were hosting a series of lectures on local history. I attended all of them, but my favorite was about this Native American who helped the police solve murder cases in the 1970s by using her spiritual gifts."

My eyes and ears were wide open. "That sounds like great material for a movie. Have you named the hero yet?"

Anna laughed. "Her name is Daisy Longtree."

I couldn't resist the urge to tease my daughter just a little bit. "So you *do* play the name game!"

And Anna quipped back. "She's a character, Mom, not an offspring!" And then she looked out over the river and was quiet again.

I sensed she was conflicted about something and scrambled to keep the conversation going. As we walked along Front Street, I nonchalantly asked, "Have you talk-ed to anyone else about this screenplay?"

"As a matter of fact, I gave it to Doris last week, and we're meeting tomorrow to talk about it. She seems genu-inely excited about it and knows someone in New York who may be interested in shopping it around for me."

Once again Anna surprised me. "Wow! That's great news! So why do you look so glum?"

"I'm not sure I'm ready to get back in the arena. Let's face it, I'm still injured."

I stopped and grabbed Anna's hand. "Oh, Anna, you were born ready. And don't let one injury sideline you."

"Thanks for the vote of confidence, Mom, but it wasn't a minor wound. Ben didn't just steal my work; he broke my heart, and he made me feel like a fool."

"You're not a fool, Anna. You were hurt by a pro!"

Anna was on the brink of crying, but she threw her head back and took a deep breath.

"I know that, but now my head has to convince my heart. Don't worry. I'll see Doris tomorrow. Who knows? Maybe this time my voice will finally be heard! Living well is the best revenge, right?"

"Yes, it is!"

And on that note, we arrived at the Blue Scone. We were both unusually quiet as we stepped inside to place our order for coffee and apricot scones. Nick was at the cash register. He hollered at us in his offbeat, sarcastic way, and Anna and I smiled, knowing that Nick would help us forget all of our worries for a little while.

"Well, if it isn't the Malone girls. What a stunning mother–daughter combination! One is bold, and the oth-er is daring."

"You must have smoke in your eyes, Nick. Check your oven!"

He feigned injury and shouted, "Ouch!"

I savored the moment. It felt good to be a regular at this cozy café. We placed our order at the counter and chatted with Tammy, the sweetest waitress in Sagadahoc County. With her short skirt, turquoise tights, and flashy bandana tied around her red hair, she added a little extra sugar to the coffee. After catching up on all the local news, Tammy handed me a brown bag with our breakfast to go, and Anna grabbed the coffees. We were about to leave when the door flew open and two men rushed in with a gust of wind. I turned away to avoid the blast of cold air, but Anna didn't, and she recognized the men right away. As I looked back over my shoulder, Nick suddenly noticed the surprise on everyone's faces and tried to add a little humor to an awkward moment.

"Look who just stumbled into my little café! If it isn't Jake Summers and Bill Marston. Good morning, gentlemen. What will it be, a Bloody Mary or an Irish coffee? Or is it still too early for adult beverages?"

While the café was buzzing with morning chatter, the four of us stood at the counter shuffling our feet in silence. Anna was the only one smiling. I suspected that the DOT's engineer and the chair of Bath's City Council were meeting to discuss the demolition of Section One, and that dampened my spirits considerably. Both men felt my icy stare. These two smart, articulate men were trying to block our efforts to stop the widening of Beacon Street. In a fog, I heard Jake's voice, and I saw Anna's eyes blink open and shut in that flirty, pretty girl way. My daughter was definitely smitten by a handsome man in a hard hat, and *my* cause was doomed to fail! As a mother, I was excited; as a community activist, I was worried. How could I defeat Maine DOT's Captain of Steel and save Bath's oldest cemetery if my daughter was falling for the enemy?

"Good morning, ladies," said Jake.

If you could taste a voice, Jake's voice tasted as smooth as a hot toddy on a cold winter's night, and I wasn't even attracted to the man!

"Hello, gentlemen. What brings you to the Blue Scone so early in the morning?" I asked rather coolly.

Bill was quick to respond. "Well, Mrs. Malone, that's an easy question. To start the day right, we need a little coffee and something more. The scones here are the best!"

"That's true, Mr. Marston, and business meetings go better with French roast and a little privacy. Have a great day!" I smiled politely and headed for the door, and Anna had the good sense to follow me without saying a word.

Outside, I took a deep breath of the crisp morning air, and let out my frustration with a hot blast. "I can't believe Bill Marston's cavalier attitude! I wonder if everyone on the City Council knows that he's meeting with Jake Summers."

Anna looked over her shoulder to see Jake sitting at a table by the window, and said, "Of course they do, Mom." She turned back to face me again. "Right now your fight may seem like the impossible dream, but don't give up. You'll find a way to make them listen. You're good at that. I mean…from time to time, *I* even listen to you."

CHAPTER 12

1881

The flower beds along Washington Street were covered with crimson and gold leaves, but some of the most royal trees were still holding onto their color. Next door to Galen Moses's mansion, a tall copper beech tree seemed to be wearing a halo of gold. According to legend, the tree had been planted in remembrance of a young child who had died. Typically, a copper beech tree wouldn't live long in cold climates, but this one showed no signs of an early demise. Many of the locals believed it was heaven-sent, and its bright October color came as a message that winter wouldn't last forever, and spring and summer would come again. Message or not, the beauty of nature gives everyone hope, and October 15, 1881, was a bright, hopeful day in Bath.

The snow-white steeple of the Winter Street Church sparkled in fresh morning light as a crowd of spectators gathered on the lawn across the street. One of the biggest weddings of the season was about to begin, and the excitement in the air was audible. The musicians had already arrived, and one could hear the violins and French horns warming up. Captain Thomas Goss was standing with his best man, Daniel McGowan, and his two grooms-men, Jeremy Gannett, his bride's younger brother, and Ephraim Hague, his friend and shipmate from *El Capitan*, on the granite steps in front of the church. They were dressed in stylish gray waistcoats, and they were laugh-ing and jabbing at each other like playful brothers. As soon as they entered the church, the crowd seemed to turn in unison to look north up Washington Street for the bride and her party. A few minutes later, two beau-tiful white carriages pulled by gleaming black horses stopped in front of the church. The first one carried the bridesmaids, and the second one carried the bride and her oldest brother, Captain Sam Gannett.

In Bath, the Gannetts were revered like royalty, and Sam Gannett was one of the most eligible bachelors in town. When his father, Colonel Frederick Gannett, was killed at the Battle of Gettysburg, Sam became the man of the house on Pearl Street and felt responsible for the well-being of his mother, younger brother, and two sisters. As he prepared to walk one of his sisters down the aisle, he smiled with happiness and relief. The church pews were filled with guests who represented every business and community organization in the city. A well-known pho-tographer from the *New York Times* had positioned him-self at the church's graceful entrance so he could capture the arrival of the local celebrities on film. This was high society at high noon, and the ladies and gentlemen of Bath were dressed in their Fifth Avenue clothes to make a statement of wealth and prosperity.

The horns began to play, and the hundreds of spec-tators gathered inside and outside of the church suddenly became quiet as the handsome young ushers helped the maid of honor and bridesmaids out of their carriage and escorted them into the vestibule of the church. Next, Cap-tain Sam Gannett stepped out of his carriage and came around to help his sister, the demure bride, step down, which was no easy task, considering the long white satin gown she was wearing had a bustle, and her corset was pulled so tight that she could barely breathe, never mind exit a carriage with grace. Once she was standing on the stone walkway, however, her fitted gown was clearly visible, and the gaping crowd sighed collectively. The bride was simply exquisite!

Inside, Thomas stood by the altar with his best man and groomsmen. While they talked casually to each other, Thomas kept glancing nervously toward the back of the church. He felt ready to pledge his devotion to Sarah in front of their family and friends, but for a fleeting moment he worried that she might not be as ready. The perspiration on his brow was beginning to slide into his eyes when he spotted Celia, the maid of honor, getting ready to walk down the aisle. He couldn't help but remember the first time he had collided, literally collided, with her aboard *El Capitan*. She had appeared so delicate with her pale skin, slender body, and mint-green eyes. But when she raised her chin, she suddenly became a pillar of strength. Her intense gaze had touched him in forbidden places. Thomas blinked hard as if to stop the memory, because now he spied his bride for the first time that morning. In the absence of her father, her brother Sam was escorting her slowly down the aisle toward the altar.

Sarah looked like a princess about to ascend the throne. Her hair was swept up with only a few blond curls cascading down her long, porcelain neck, and a silver comb, something old, held her long veil of Flemish lace perfectly in place. Her waist couldn't have been any smaller, and her bustle couldn't have been more stylish. Thomas drank her beauty in like sweet wine. Sarah was breathtaking.

As soon as Captain Gannett lifted his sister's veil and gave her a parting kiss on the cheek, Thomas stepped forward to offer her his arm. Sunlight streamed in through the tall church windows, and the organ played as Sarah and Thomas climbed three steps to stand in front of the minister. Charlotte and Henry were sitting in the first pew with a clear view of the angelic, fair-haired bride and the handsome, dark-haired groom. Henry took hold of Charlotte's hand, pulled it over to touch his own heart, kissed it gently, and set it down again on the folds of her blue gown. Charlotte tried to slow her own breathing. She was surprised by how nervous she felt, and she couldn't help but notice how the minister was staring at Sarah's breasts. She wondered if others noticed the object of Reverend Mitchell's focus. Sarah's tight corset was obviously pushing up her bounty, and the holy reverend could not seem to take his eyes off of them. Charlotte, far less endowed, looked down at her own breasts and wondered if the old saying was true. Could Thomas find lasting happiness with such a fetching wife?

Neither Henry nor Charlotte seemed to hear the vows that were being spoken at that moment before the eyes of God; rather, both of them worried that their son might be entering into a family that was too rich, too powerful, and too beautiful.

Before the entire Winter Street Church congregation, Thomas bent down to kiss his bride. His lips, fervent and parted, covered Sarah's rosebud mouth, but her lips did not surrender. For the photographer standing ten feet away, it was a perfect kiss, but it was too shallow and quick for Thomas's hot blood. Charlotte, sitting in the front row, felt a chill from that short kiss. As the French horns began to play, she wondered if the fairy-tale wedding was simply an illusion.

Celia saw the flicker of imperfection as well, and a heavy sigh escaped her soul. From the core of her being, Celia knew that Thomas was marrying the wrong Gannett. She feared that Sarah was simply too beautiful to be caring and giving as a wife. Later, she worried that Daniel McGowan, her escort, might have heard her woeful sigh.

But despite Celia's fear and Charlotte's concern, Mr. and Mrs. Thomas Goss walked down the aisle arm in arm with bright smiles.

Once outside, Thomas looked for his parents, and as soon as he found them, he embraced them both. "Could you tell I was sweating?"

"No, you looked calm and in love!" Charlotte kissed his cheek and whispered, "We wish you and Sarah every happiness!"

Henry wrapped his left arm around Thomas and patted him on the back, and then he handed Thomas two envelopes. "These are wedding gifts. One envelope is from Galen Moses, and you should open that one first. He and his family have been kind and generous neighbors. The second envelope is from a few of your rowing friends at Bowdoin, and you should open that tonight. I was asked to deliver both gifts as soon as you tied the knot."

Thomas looked at his father and said, "I feel so blessed today."

"Congratulations, Son, you just tied the strongest sailor's knot imaginable! May you and Sarah enjoy a long and happy life together! And there is one more gift, and this one is from your mother and me."

Charlotte gave Thomas a small blue-velvet bag tied with a white satin ribbon, and Henry handed him a small wooden box.

Thomas swallowed hard before responding. "You've already given us so much."

Henry cleared his throat. "The bag contains your grandmother's silver brooch, and the box contains your grandfather's pocket watch."

"Thank you," said Thomas. "Sarah and I will cherish these gifts." He kissed his mother and reached for his father's hand. "Father, I hope I can be as good a husband to Sarah as you have been to Mother."

"All you have to do, Thomas, is keep loving her."

Sarah approached the three of them and smiled

sweetly. "It's hard to believe I was Sarah Gannett an hour ago, and now I am Sarah Goss."

"Well, welcome to the family, my dear," said Henry in a booming voice while Charlotte gave her a big hug.

While everyone was hugging, Thomas stepped aside to open the first envelope. "What's this?" he asked as he held up a key.

"Read the note," answered Henry.

Dear Thomas,

Our families have been friends for more years than I can count, and I believe my father would be displeased with me if I did not add to the splendor of your wedding day, so I am offering you the key to our home on Washington Street. You can begin your honeymoon tonight. Our largest guest room has been pre-pared for you, and you won't be disturbed. My wife and I are spending the night at our summer house. I am also sending my finest carriage and swiftest team of horses to carry you and Mrs. Goss up the street. Today you deserve royal transportation!

Best wishes,
Galen C. Moses and family

"I'm speechless. This is beyond generous. It is the perfect gift, and it is life-saving because I have been so pre-occupied with the wedding day that I didn't plan for the wedding night! I guess I thought Daniel would take care of all that, but knowing Daniel that was probably foolish!"

By now, Sam, Jeremy, and Celia Gannett had joined the circle along with Sarah's bridesmaids, and they were all looking over Thomas's shoulder and laughing heartily.

"Let me guess: Daniel is standing behind me," said Thomas.

"Why of course, darling," said Sarah, blushing.

Daniel seized the moment to have some fun with his old friend. "I don't think you'll find me lacking in social grace when you open the second envelope. In fact, I can spare you the trouble of opening it and just tell you what I have planned for you."

"Oh, please do," said Thomas with a chuckle.

"Your boat mates from Bowdoin, including me, have arranged for you and Sarah to spend five nights at the New York City Athletic Club at Central Park South. It was John Caverly's idea. Lucky for us, he became a member to train for the next summer Olympics. We all thought you and Sarah would enjoy the club's fine accommodations and excellent location."

Thomas reached out to shake Daniel's hand. "I don't know how to thank you."

Daniel smiled. "Your seven Bowdoin brothers wish you and Sarah every blessing. Your train leaves at noon tomorrow. Don't be late!"

The circle was quiet. Even Sarah seemed genuinely touched by such a generous and thoughtful gift.

Thomas cleared his throat and struggled to find the right words. "Daniel, my brothers in rowing will always be dear to me. I remember with fondness every hour we spent on the water together! But my left shoulder still aches when it rains!"

Thomas gave Daniel a back-slapping hug, and everyone laughed. Charlotte pulled her mother's handkerchief from the sleeve of her dress. It was the first time she had needed that sentimental piece of lace all day.

Gradually, the guests began to stroll over to the church hall, where twenty round tables were covered with white linen and set with fine flint glassware, sterling silver, and Haviland china. On every table were ceramic vases shaped like mermaids, seahorses, and treasure chests filled with purple, yellow, and white chrysanthemums. Next to the dance floor at the back of the hall was a baby grand piano, a harp, and a group of musicians in formal attire. Only the violinists were playing as the guests entered and looked for their seats. The best cooks in Bath were downstairs in the kitchen preparing salmon, roast duck, whipped potatoes, and a cornucopia of fruits and vegetables. It was only one o'clock in the afternoon, but the servers were busy placing bottles of red and white wine on each table and pouring tall glasses of champagne for everyone present. Shortly after Sarah and Thomas sat down at the head table, Daniel McGowan rose to toast the bride and groom.

"Let's raise our glasses and wish long life and many children to Thomas, my oldest friend and greatest rival, and Sarah, the beautiful woman I lusted for, but lost to Thomas!"

"Hear! Hear!" shouted Jeremy. "And let me add that the best man won!"

With that announcement, the hall erupted into laughter, and the musicians began to play a waltz, which called the newlyweds and their party to the dance floor. As soon as Sarah and Thomas twirled around the floor twice, the rest of the bridal party began to dance, and the dance floor remained full until the music stopped. The Gannett family had transformed the modest church hall into a grand ballroom, and every lady and gentleman in attendance wanted to hold someone in his or her arms and glide about the floor. As the party continued, dancers began to change partners, and Thomas found himself dancing with his new sister-in-law. She was pressed tightly to his chest, and he could smell her hair. Her scent was strangely familiar, and it encouraged him to speak.

"Thank you, Celia. I know you were the one who made this day look and feel divine. You have the touch of an artist, and that is heaven-sent."

"You're welcome," replied Celia. "Sarah is my only sister, and I want us to remain close, which means I will be close to you, too."

With that double-edged comment hanging in the air, a stranger cut in and begged to dance with Celia. Thomas stepped off the dance floor and headed for the bar. It was time for whiskey, not wine.

One hour later, Galen Moses's handsome carriage, pulled by two dramatic white horses, stopped in front of the Winter Street Church. Thomas placed his two hands around Sarah's slender waist and lifted her up to the back seat; then he jumped in beside her and flashed his winning smile to the almost two hundred guests who stood watching from the broad lawn and the wide-open doors of the church hall. The hour to consummate the marriage had come, and Thomas was eager to say goodbye to his guests so that he could properly say hello to Mrs. Thomas Goss!

As they rode off with cans clanging from the back of the carriage, only his mother questioned whether he had won a beautiful woman for the night, or a loving wife for a lifetime.

CHAPTER 13

2014

Soft, downy flakes were falling when I stepped outside to take Freckles for her morning walk. Every day, we head to Section One of the Beacon Hill Cemetery at seven o'clock. I like to visit the sleeping sea captains and their loved ones. Sometimes, when I pass by their tombstones, I read their names aloud as if I'm studying them in a history class. After all, our City of Ships would not exist without the vision and valor of the men and women laid to rest on Beacon Hill.

Tonight, the Bath City Council would be meeting to decide the fate of Section One. Hopefully, the members would decide to do the right thing and vote to save the oldest part of our cemetery. Standing inside the iron gates, surrounded by tall oaks and towering maples, my heart told me that wisdom would prevail. And just as I felt a lightness within me for the first time in months, I heard a voice calling my name.

"Mrs. Malone? Mrs. Malone, is that you?" the husky voice called through the blowing wind and frosty air.

I turned to see Jake Summers approaching. He was walking a Great Pyrenees—or perhaps it was the other way around, because the dog seemed to be dragging him toward Freckles and me with incredible force.

"Let me guess. You believe bigger is better!" I called back. And then I prayed that my little dachshund-sheltie would survive the meeting that was about to happen.

Jake waited to reply until he was standing directly in front of me. As he wrestled with getting his excited dog to sit, I was struck by the poetry of our position in the cemetery. We were standing next to the grave of Oliver Moses, one of Bath's most important developers in the nineteenth century. He and his brother William had arrived in Bath in 1826 and established the city's first foundry on the west side of Front Street. Years later, the Moses brothers sold their Bath Iron Foundry to General Thomas Hyde, who ultimately became the president of Bath Iron Works. I couldn't help but feel that heavenly forces were aligning to save Bath's legendary graveyard.

"No, bigger isn't always better," said Jake with a teasing smile. "Moose, however, *is* big, and he's the right dog for me." He looked down at Freckles and Moose doing the circle dance and said, "Opposites really do attract!"

Without a doubt, Jake recognized the irony of our accidental meeting on Beacon Hill, and he quickly seized the opportunity to initiate a friendly conversation. I had to give him points for trying.

"Whoa!" I said. "Strong and charming is a dangerous combination."

Jake turned red from the neck up.

"I'm sorry, Mrs. Malone. I'll try not to put anyone you know at risk."

"Oh, I think it's too late for that," I said with a grin. "And call me Ellie. 'Mrs. Malone' is way too formal!"

"Ellie, I hope you know I'm not happy about bulldozing sacred ground and destroying monuments. I wonder if the summer bottlenecks are really that unbearable." Jake bent down and ran his hand over Moose's soft coat. Almost inaudibly, he whispered, "I ask myself that a lot lately."

I looked down at my orange boots, dusted with snow, and reflected for a long moment on Jake's openness. He seemed so genuine.

"That's my question, too," I finally said with a sigh.

Freckles tugged a bit at her leash before she realized we were officially stopped, and then she sat down next to Moose. Suddenly, these two fast friends reminded me of the two main characters in *The Rocky and Bullwinkle Show*, and I laughed.

I looked at Jake, and I couldn't help but notice his profoundly blue eyes. "Would you mind if we walked down the trail a bit together? I think our furry companions are waiting for us to choose a direction."

Jake smiled. "Let's keep moving. I think we're making progress."

We continued down the winding path toward the west side of the cemetery. The morning sun felt good on my back. It was a perfect day for a winter walk, but we didn't go a hundred yards before Jake decided to stop, and Moose came to an abrupt halt right beside him. Of course, that meant Freckles and I had to stop, too. We were all standing still in a patch of woods that was lit up like a cathedral by rays of sunshine streaming through the bare branches of a big oak tree.

"Ellie," Jake said in a quiet voice, "is it possible for you and me to come up with a plan that would honor the sea captains and founding families who are buried here on Beacon Hill *and* satisfy Maine DOT and the City Council?"

"I believe anything is possible if you put your heart and soul into it."

Jake finally stood at ease. "In that case, I think I know how to please almost everyone—the DOT, the City Council, the good people of Bath, and even the motorists along Route 1—if you are willing to present my plan as your own tonight."

I cocked an eyebrow at him. "Am I understanding this correctly? You want me to carry your plan to City Hall and fervently request that the City Council consider it without letting anyone know that you created it."

"Exactly!" Jake said with a winning smile spreading across his rugged, handsome face.

"Okay, but you and I are going over to see Doris right now, and we're going to review this plan all together."

* * *

Twelve hours later, Jake and I met again, but this time we were not standing next to each other—we were across the aisle from each other at City Hall. Bill Marston was getting ready to call the meeting to order by pounding his gavel on the mahogany table, which stood on a raised platform. It was 6:59 p.m. and every seat in the hall was taken. Doris was sitting directly behind me. She put her hand on my shoulder, leaned forward, and whispered a few encouraging words.

"You've got this, Ellie!"

As my eyes nervously scanned the room, I thought I saw every shopkeeper and business owner in Bath, as well as all of my friends from NPI. I couldn't help but wonder why Jake, with all of his military experience, thought I was the best person to present his proposal. From my front-row seat, I looked back with trepidation at scores of unsmiling people. All of them seemed anxious and ready to fight. When I tried to focus on the pages of notes in my hand, my dinner started doing somersaults, so I decided to put my notes away. I carefully slid them back into my green folder and placed the folder at my feet. With a deep cleansing breath, I tried to steady my nerves. Since I was a seasoned high school teacher, I knew I could speak convincingly in front of a large group, but I wasn't sure I had the verbal power to persuade a crowd of angry Mainers.

On our morning walk, Jake had disagreed with me. His combat experience had taught him that sometimes strong, passionate men are not the best peacemakers. Mothers and teachers, on the other hand, are skilled at resolving conflict. Jake firmly believed that I was the best person to present a compromise that would satisfy both the business community and the citizens in favor of historic preservation. The notes in my folder were actually the summary of a document Jake had sent to me that afternoon. Our plan offered the City of Bath an olive branch.

I could hear the sound of Bill Marston's gavel less than six feet in front of me, and I was ready to stand up and speak, but I knew that old business was listed first on the agenda. Councilman Peter Day reported on several beautification and restoration projects as the crowded room grew fidgety.

I glanced back at the tall, ornately carved doors at the back of the hall and spied Anna and Ty making a last-minute entrance. Anna had picked Ty up at the Portland airport and brought him straight to the meeting. As soon as they spotted me, they came down and quickly filled the seats next to mine. Ty kissed my cheek and grabbed my hand. His warm, chocolate-brown eyes told me everything would be okay.

"Let's get this show on the road," he said, and then he leaned in for a full kiss.

I suddenly heard my name being read aloud. Bill Marston was introducing me as the next speaker on the agenda.

Softly, so only Ty could hear, I whispered, "Show time!"

Slowly, I let go of Ty's hand, stood up, and faced the City Council.

"Good evening! I am grateful for this opportunity to speak on behalf of those who cannot—the souls buried in Section One of the Beacon Hill Cemetery. Tonight we can choose to preserve the memory of our founding families, the shipbuilders and sea captains who forged our history, by agreeing to delay the destruction of Section One until the bodies buried there can be properly exhumed, the remains cremated, and the ashes placed in a memorial garden. Friends, the ship *Dirigo* was built in Bath. Its name means 'I lead,' and that also happens to be our state motto. Let's make sure Bath leads in preserving Maine's maritime history!"

A few dissenters in the crowd started to grumble. I decided to turn and face them, but first I glanced at Ty and Anna. When I saw that Anna was videotaping the meeting, I immediately felt empowered. My family was in my corner, and I was ready for the fight.

"Please hear me out. This new idea will surprise you. If we agree to implement it, we will see change in the best possible way."

Bill Marston pounded his gavel and shouted, "Quiet in the hall!" Then he peered down at me from his lofty chair and said, "Okay, Mrs. Malone, you have our undivided attention."

"Before proceeding with their road improvement plan, Maine DOT needs to exhume, not bulldoze, the graves that will be affected by the new construction. Every preservationist here today realizes that landscapes must change with the passing of time. The issue here is not the changing landscape, the loss of trees and green space; rather, it is the loss of our human history, the proof that we inhabited this land and paved the roads we still travel on today. The tombstones on Beacon Hill prove that we nurtured our families here with joy and sorrow, laughter and tears. If progress requires us to bulldoze those tombstones, we must exhume the bodies first, and we must find a new place where our forefathers and -mothers can rest in peace. There has to be a compromise."

John Coffin, usually the quietest member of the City Council, posed a question. "Where would that place be, and how much would all this cost?"

I answered with confidence. "We can cremate the remains and scatter the ashes."

Out of the corner of my eye, I saw Jake lean over to

whisper something in his boss's ear. And then the director of the DOT, Mr. Richard Lane, stood up to respond.

"If we cremate the remains, the cost will be reasonable. Do you have a specific place in mind for scattering the ashes?"

"Yes, I do, Mr. Lane." I noticed my hands were sweating, but my voice was strong and steady. "In the 1980s, the parish of Saint Mary's Catholic Church deeded the Calvary Cemetery at the corner of Whiskeag Road and High Street to the City of Bath. There are only thirty-two graves there, but the oldest dates back to 1899. That piece of land is rich with history, and there's a lot of open space around it. I can imagine a memorial center surrounded by flower beds. We could have our landscapers build a stone wall for remembering the important men and women who built our city, and they could also make a walkway of large, smooth stones. I think we could engrave the stones with the names of our heroes as well as their birth and death years. Perhaps we could even include their most significant contributions to Bath's history."

I picked up the green folder, handed it to Bill, who was still sitting behind the grand table at the front of the hall, and began my closing remarks.

"Members of the Council, this folder contains a detailed description of the plan I have just outlined. It's the best compromise we could imagine. Please consider it and approve it as soon as possible."

I stopped talking and the silent crowd broke into thunderous applause. I looked over to see both Jake and his boss standing up and clapping with big grins that all but shouted, *That's a deal!*

"Well, Ellie, by the sound of that applause, I think you've done it!" said Bill as he rapped his gavel triumphantly on the table.

A few minutes later, he came over to shake my hand. "We will have to study the plan and meet with Maine DOT, but I don't think you have much to worry about. Quite frankly, you've designed a beautiful way of honoring our history. I've always thought that Calvary Cemetery is one of the most peaceful places in Bath. You've picked a sweet spot! Thank you, Ellie!"

Doris shouted, "Hooray!" and gave me a hug. Then she stepped back and softly said, "Ellie, my dear, you make impossible things happen!"

"No," I said, "*we* did this! Tonight's victory belongs to Team Bath!"

Everyone was standing and chatting with their neighbors. It felt like Memorial Day and the Fourth of July all rolled into one, but I did feel a twinge of guilt. The plan really belonged to Jake. It wasn't mine. I wanted to rush over and give him a big bear hug, but before I could take a step in his direction, he approached me.

"Ellie," he half shouted, "you saved a lot of souls tonight by sharing yours. Well done!"

"Oh, my goodness, Mr. Summers. You really do know how to give a girl a compliment. Now, I suggest you go over and talk to my daughter. Perhaps you haven't noticed, but she has been looking at you all night, and I haven't seen her eyes dance like that in a long time."

Jake laughed out loud, and it was a thunderous sound that seemed to rock the space around us. As he turned to look at Anna, I invited him to our house for a victory party.

"On my way to the meeting tonight, I stopped at the market and bought a few bottles of champagne because I really do believe in miracles! You should help us uncork those bottles, Jake. The victory is really yours! You know where we live, right?"

"Yes," Jake said with a grin, "I think I know where you live. But just to play it safe, I'll ask Anna for directions."

I laughed and said, "You're quite an operator, Mr. Summers. I'll see you and Anna at the house." Then I waved and headed toward the exit.

As I waited for Ty, who was busy talking with a neighbor, I thought about Jake's amazing plan. He was the one who deserved the applause. Earlier that day, when we met with Doris, I had a chance to see Jake in a different light. He was a man with many layers, but beneath them all there was a caring heart and a creative mind, and I admired his character even more than his good looks.

Less than an hour later, Ty and I were greeting guests at our home on Washington Street. We were standing at the foot of the stairs when Doris Van der Waag walked through the front door, followed by a bunch of thoroughly delighted NPI board members. Trailing behind, and secretly hoping that no one would notice, Anna and Jake slipped in the side door. Our big old house filled up quickly, and there were clusters of happy people everywhere, especially in the kitchen, which was Anna and Jake's point of entry. Doris's radar fixed on the fact that they arrived together, and she gave them both a quick hug.

"Thank you, Jake," said Doris. "Ellie tells me the credit for the memorial garden idea goes to you. It seems you're not only a talented engineer, but a brilliant mediator as well!"

Jake whispered back, "Please, Mrs. Van der Waag, don't share that intel with my boss. He might question where my true allegiance lies."

Doris laughed. "Don't worry. Your secret is safe with me."

At some point when I wasn't looking, Jake and Anna made a quick getaway.

* * *

On the deck outside the sliding glass doors of the sunroom, Jake wrapped one arm around Anna's waist. Together they leaned over the railing to view the stars over the Kennebec. Jake pointed to the North Star.

"I always like to find the North Star. For me, it's a comforting sight."

"That's funny because my parents call me their North Star."

"Really? Why?"

"When I was working in the film industry, I had to travel a lot, and my parents liked to follow me."

"Tell me, Anna, why is a pretty girl like you still on the market?" asked Jake.

"I'm not sure how to answer that."

Jake looked directly at Anna with his intense eyes and said, "When in doubt, just tell the truth."

"You're right, but it's a long story," she said with a trembling voice. Then she looked up, scanned the night sky, and tried to steady her nerves. "In the interest of time, let me just say that I stayed too long at the fair with the wrong guy."

"So was this your Hollywood leading man?"

"No, he wasn't a leading man, but he was a powerful man. He stole my work, and he almost stole my voice."

Jake pulled her closer. "Have I told you how beautifully you craft your words?"

Anna giggled as she leaned into him. "I craft a lot of things well. Let me show you."

On that playful note, Anna reached up and kissed him on the cheek and then on the mouth, and the world slipped into silence for a long, lingering moment. In fact, the kiss seemed to play a trick with time, making it seem like forever. When the two had finally exhausted all of their air, their lips parted. Anna leaned back and looked up at Jake's clean-shaven face. His chiseled good looks reminded her of every movie star she had ever swooned over as a teenager. Jake looked like the quintessential American hero, and she could feel her heart pounding beneath her soft, lamb's-wool sweater.

"It's my turn to ask a personal question," she said with a teasing grin. "Why is a Herculean guy like you still available at...what, thirty-five?"

"Make that thirty-seven, and in a word, the answer is Fallujah. I haven't been easy to be with since coming back. It's been a long road for me to get back to the land of the living."

Jake leaned out over the railing and searched the sky again for the North Star. "Look!" he cried with a boyish exuberance. He pulled Anna close and pointed to the dark sky illuminated by stars. "There's Orion, one of the brightest constellations. That bright red star is Betelgeuse, and it marks Orion's left shoulder. The blue-white star there is called Rigel; it marks his right foot."

"Wait. Where's the foot?"

Jake slipped behind Anna and gently lifted her arm to point it in Rigel's direction. "There! Do you see it?" he asked quietly.

Anna felt his breath. She swallowed hard before answering. "Yes!"

With his hand over hers, he traced a line. "That row of three stars forms his belt, and the fainter, dangling stars form his sword."

Jake's extensive knowledge of astronomy took Anna by surprise. "How do you know so much about Orion?" she asked.

"Well, I may be an engineer, but physics and mathematics were not the only subjects I studied. According to Greek mythology, Orion was a hunter, a giant who had the power to walk through the sea and on its surface, but he had a troubled love life."

Jake paused and placed his hands on the railing. His mood had suddenly changed, and Anna noticed. She linked her arm in his and gently teased, "Doesn't everyone have trouble with their love life?"

He turned and looked directly into her eyes. "No, not everyone," he said. And then he bent down and placed his mouth over her soft lips and kissed her long and hard before continuing.

With one arm still around her waist, he quietly told her the rest of the story. "Orion had a talent for angering gods and goddesses alike, and many tried to harm him. Ultimately, Artemis, the goddess of hunters, killed Orion with an arrow while he was swimming. Later, she regretted her decision, and, in her sorrow, placed Orion in the sky as a constellation to shine for all eternity."

Looking up at the night sky, Anna understood the depth of Artemis's sorrow. She shivered, and Jake pulled her closer. It was cold on the deck. Suddenly, the twinkle lights in the rafters, and the moon and stars above, weren't enough to keep them warm. Orion's tragic story had definitely affected Anna. At that moment, she appeared distant, and Jake sensed her loneliness. He pressed his face into her curly dark hair and breathed in her scent. He kissed her gently on the ear, the cheek, and finally the mouth. And all the sadness of their combined history disappeared.

When they came up for air, Jake had an important question to ask. "So, would you like to go on a date with me? I think Mike and Marty's in Brunswick makes the best Manhattan in the state of Maine, and their entrees are excellent, too."

"Yes, I would like that. When?"

"Tomorrow night at seven?" Then he chuckled, "Even that seems too long to wait."

Anna grabbed his hand, and as they stepped inside, they started to laugh, and that happy sound certainly reached Orion, because the stars winked at them as they left the deck.

CHAPTER 14

1884

Tucked safely inside Charlotte and Henry Goss's charming home on Washington Street, Sarah sat rocking her four-month-old baby girl, Lily, while Celia played the piano and softly sang a Scottish folk song that their mother used to sing. The lyrics were sad because they described a young boy leaving home and going to sea for the first time, but the music was soothing. Sarah started to sing along, her high soprano voice blending perfectly with her sister's warm alto notes, and Lily stretched in her arms. As darkness fell, the lullaby's sweet refrain filled the house with peace.

When it was clear that Lily was sound asleep, Celia stood up and stepped away from the piano. She picked up her needlework, a birth sampler for Lily, and sat down on the settee in front of the fire. Sarah got up and gently placed her sleeping infant in the cradle beside the rocking chair, then quickly sat down again, happy to have a quiet moment to visit with Celia. For a new mother, she was doing remarkably well and seemed content to pass most of her days nursing and changing the newest member of the family.

"I know some women become dreadfully sad after childbirth," Sarah confided, "but I have never felt so fulfilled and blessed as I do right now."

"That is clear to everyone who sees you! My dear, you're radiant! Motherhood suits you, and Thomas is a lucky man. Speaking of Thomas, where is the dashing young captain? I haven't seen him, or his illustrious father, this evening."

"At the shipyard, of course," Sarah answered with a sigh. "Please don't repeat this, but I think the shipyard is in trouble. Thomas doesn't like to discuss business with me, but he has been worried for quite some time about how much money Henry and his partners have invested in steam auxiliaries. A lot of shipbuilders call it the great maritime experiment."

Slightly alarmed, Celia stopped stitching and looked up at Sarah. "I've heard rumblings of a possible downturn for the shipbuilders, but Henry's yard has been called Bath's 'factory.' I had no idea his company was in trouble. How long have you known?"

"It's been brewing for a while. Do you remember when I accompanied Thomas to Buenos Aires on the steam bark *Mendoza* shortly after we were married?"

"Yes. How could I forget! You were as nervous as a schoolgirl getting ready for her first dance."

Sarah blushed and continued in a more serious tone. "Well, while we were planning our trip, Thomas confided in me his concern over his father's investment in steam. He felt it was a risky business."

Celia listened in awe as her once carefree sister tried to explain how steam was supposed to reduce travel time by a third, thereby allowing a bark commissioned for the South American wool trade to make three voyages a year. But that was not always the case. In 1882, the *Mendoza* had only made two successful voyages from New York to Buenos Aires because of weather.

"When did my little sister become so interested in

the family business?" Celia teased. "I didn't realize you were following maritime trade so closely. Your knowledge is quite impressive!"

"I don't think it's the business that interests me; it's Thomas's well-being. I see how the stress affects him. He is such a loving, good man, but sometimes his mood darkens and he becomes withdrawn. When that happens, I cannot seem to lift his spirits."

"You can always talk to me," Celia said as she stood up and walked over to the windows to look out on the snow-covered street. "Tell me more about the *Mendoza*. I'm intrigued."

Sarah took a deep breath. She looked over at Lily, who was fast asleep, and then she let her mind drift back to that dreadful passage. The *Mendoza* never reached Buenos Aires that winter. She had left Bath on December 4, 1882. After a two-day snowstorm wreaked havoc on her engine, she lost power for eighteen hours. Because she was lightly ballasted, she was driven out to sea. Days later, she found a safe port at Saint Thomas in the Virgin Islands. The exhausted crew loaded on a hundred tons of additional stone ballast before departing for New York on December 29, but the *Mendoza* hit heavy weather again, and her arrival in New York was delayed until January 14, 1883.

"Celia, I have never felt more terrified than I was on that stormy passage from Bath to New York, nor have I ever felt more grateful than the moment I spied New York's harbor glistening in snow and ice!"

A hush filled the room, and then the fire crackled, and Sarah stood up and joined her sister at the window just as the gas lamps were being lit along Washington Street.

"You know," said Sarah, "in New York City the streets are lined with electric lights."

Celia replied in a quiet voice, "Don't worry; Bath will have electric lights soon. Everything changes in time, and yet everything remains oddly the same. Look! It's starting to snow again."

In unison, they pushed the lace curtains aside and gazed in awe at the falling snowflakes on the other side of the glass. "When you're safe inside a warm, cozy house, snow is truly beautiful, isn't it?" Sarah mused.

"Yes, freshly fallen snow offers everyone a new beginning," said Celia, and turning toward her sister, she asked, "Why did you wait so long to tell me about your frightening ordeal on the *Mendoza*?"

Sarah looked directly at her sister and said, "I didn't want to complain about my life as a sea captain's wife. I thought you didn't approve of my decision to marry Thomas. You told me I was too young, and I didn't know him well enough to make such a serious commitment. Your words haunt me to this day. Maybe you were right. I was young, but I was also in love. Looking back, I'm afraid I wasn't a glowing bride because I was trying so hard to be refined and sophisticated. For Thomas's sake, I wish I had shown more emotion that day."

With a twinge of guilt, Celia felt a chill travel up her spine. Sarah was right. She had disapproved of the marriage, but not because Sarah was too young. The reason was far more selfish than that, but clearly not apparent to her sister.

"I'm sorry, Sarah. I didn't realize how strong and certain your heart truly is. You're braver than I ever imagined."

Sarah grabbed Celia's hand and said, "I'm glad you're here. I'm really not that brave, and that little baby stirring in her cradle over there frightens me more than gusting winds at sea."

As Lily let out her first real cry of the evening, Celia gave Sarah a quick hug before letting her go. "You comfort Lily. I'll rummage through the pantry and see what I can pull together for supper."

"You read my mind. I'm as hungry as Lily most of the time! I think you'll find a pot of stew on the stove. And if I know my mother-in-law, there's also a tray of homemade biscuits waiting in the pantry."

"Is Charlotte visiting her family in Riggsville today?" Celia asked.

"Yes, Amy took a bad fall, and the recovery has been slow and painful. Charlotte is now the matriarch of the family, and she frets about everyone. Thank heaven she has so much energy. I can only hope that I grow old as gracefully as she."

"The Goss and Riggs families are kind and generous, Sarah. You are twice blessed."

"Why, Celia, I am three times blessed. The Gannetts are good people, too!"

Celia weighed her words and said, "Well, I'm sure some of us are good."

As Sarah cradled Lily in her arms and swayed gently from side to side, she asked the logical question, "And who is supposed to be so bad?"

Celia's tone became more serious as she lowered her telling eyes and said, "Some people think our brother, Sam, was cruel. You know he had a fierce temper. I know it's wrong to speak ill of the dead, but Sarah, even I was afraid of him."

Just as Sarah was about to respond, the front door blew open and Thomas and his father entered with a gust of cold wind.

Thomas said, "Hello, my dears!" and bent down to undo his boots.

As he stood up, he pulled off his wool cap and a shock of curly brown hair was set loose. Celia hurried over to take the men's heavy coats, and she hung them carefully on the big wrought-iron hooks of the costumer standing in the corner of the entranceway. Thomas smiled and gave her a kiss on the cheek, and Celia felt herself blush, so she quickly turned and hurried down the hall to the kitchen.

Glancing back toward the door, Celia said in an unusually high voice, "I was just about to put supper on the table. Your timing couldn't be better."

"Don't hurry. I need a warm hug before I can eat. My face feels frozen and only my beautiful wife and my sweet baby girl can melt it!" Thomas laughed and buried his cold cheeks in Sarah's soft curls. Celia swallowed hard and banged a few pots around so as not to hear another cheerful word.

Less than an hour later, Henry, Thomas, Sarah, and Celia sat around the dining room table while Lily slept in her cradle. The stew disappeared quickly, and Thomas ate the last biscuit without a hint of guilt. The hearty home-cooked meal cast a comforting spell over the group. When Henry pushed back ever so slightly from the table, Celia seized the moment to ask about his day.

"How is business at the shipyard, Henry?"

Henry hesitated before answering. "If you are asking how my crews are doing, they are doing excellent work. I believe the most skilled workmen in Bath work for us, and I have no complaints about the yard, but if you are asking how business is, well then my answer is quite different."

"Why Captain Goss, that sounds like a problem wrapped in a riddle!" Celia was trying to be lighthearted, but she was concerned and continued to press for a more definitive answer. "Whatever do you mean?"

"I need to tell you about some changes that are coming. The truth is that Thomas and I did not spend all day at the shipyard. At about three o'clock we walked down to Galen Moses's office to meet with a group of investors. Next month, the firm of Goss and Sawyer, will become the New England Shipbuilding Company. I will at least continue to serve as a member of the board of directors, but it is a difficult change."

After Henry's somber announcement, the only sound was Lily's quiet breathing until Thomas asked for a slice of his mother's apple pie.

"I think we could all use some of mother's apple goodness right now."

Celia jumped out of her chair, and said, "I'll bring

everyone a huge piece with lots of whipped cream."

"I'll help!" said Sarah as she stood up and followed her sister through the pantry door and into the kitchen.

Once they reached the kitchen and were out of listening range, Celia set the pie on the sideboard, Sarah spread out four dessert plates, and the two sisters began to discuss their next move. A simple glance between them made clear that neither planned to stay out of the family business for one more minute.

As Celia cut the pie with a sharp knife and a steady hand, she told Sarah about her recent visit to the family's attorney.

"Yesterday, Mr. Stinson informed me that we own sizable shares in two ships, *El Capitan* and the *Paul Revere*, and our inheritance from Sam is more substantial than we thought. We also own an interest in one of Uncle Arthur's future projects, the *Susquehanna*."

Sarah looked genuinely surprised. "I know so little about our investments, but I do remember our voyage on *El Capitan*. It was more romantic than I ever expected!"

Celia shook her head and laughed. "Oh, Sarah, you were always looking for romance. Perhaps that's why you found it. But I have often wondered why Sam invited us on that voyage. He rarely showed us any affection or expressed any interest in our well-being. I wonder if he had an ulterior motive. I know Thomas fell in love with you within a month of leaving port! Do you think Sam was playing matchmaker?"

"I doubt our brother was ever that romantic, but I'm grateful for the opportunity he offered us, and it seems he is still taking care of the family from his grave. Don't you think Sam would want Thomas to take over command of *El Capitan*?"

"Yes, I believe Sam would be in favor of it. He told me once that no smarter captain ever sailed out of Bath than Thomas. He thought he was an outstanding navigator and forecaster of weather. My fear is that *El Capitan* is a troubled ship. Sam's death may not have been an accident."

"That's a dark suspicion, Celia. Look on the bright side! Uncle Arthur sold his shares of *El Capitan* to De-Groote and Peck. Thomas would be sailing under a new flag, and that can change a ship's luck. *El Capitan* will be successful, and we will be able to help the whole family weather these hard times."

Celia shook her head and smiled. "When did my little sister become so wise and hopeful?"

"The day I gave birth to Lily," said Sarah matter-of-factly.

"Okay then, I will visit Uncle Arthur's office tomor-row, and I'll ask him to convince the new owners to offer the command of *El Capitan* to Thomas."

With that decision made, Celia and Sarah carried the pie into the dining room just in time to see Thomas pouring four glasses of whiskey.

"Make that three glasses," Sarah told Thomas with a lilt in her voice. "Someone has to comfort Lily when she wakes up at two in the morning!"

"Ah, that is so true," answered Thomas. "And we know it won't be me!"

CHAPTER 15

2014

We were having lunch at Faye's, *the* place to order a grilled turkey and cheddar panini with cranberry chutney, when Jake called. I knew it was Jake because Anna's voice suddenly climbed to a high soprano. I smiled as I remembered how my sons always dropped their voices from tenor to baritone whenever a girl called. Everything changes, and everything remains the same.

When Anna put her phone down, I decided to test the water. "It sounds like you and Jake are planning a trip."

"Mom, you love to read into things. I think *you're* the wild gypsy in the family, not me."

"I don't need a crystal ball to see how you feel about the guy who makes you giggle like a schoolgirl. Could you at least tell me where you and Jake will be spending the weekend?"

Anna lowered her eyes as she fidgeted with her phone and considered an exit strategy, but after a long pause she answered. "We're going to drive down to Worcester to see the New England Rowing Championships. Jake follows collegiate rowing. Who knew! And he was impressed when I told him my brother rowed for Holy Cross."

As I listened to Anna talk about Holy Cross and rowing regattas, I wondered where my artsy daughter had gone. To my knowledge, Anna had only attended one of Joe's crew races during the four years he rowed in college. Once, at Christmas dinner, she had asked Joe why he was so committed to the crew team. Joe simply said he liked boats, and he could study better when he was physically exhausted. And then I think he asked Anna to pass him the stuffing. The memory held me captive for a moment.

"I'm sorry, but did you just say you were going to a regatta with Jake?"

"That's exactly what I said. Why?"

"It just surprises me that you're going to a regatta and not a movie."

"I know, but I think it's neat that Jake is a fan of a sport my family loves. And that's why I invited Joe and Frank to watch the races with us. I'm hoping they like Jake. If they don't, I would rather find that out before we get more involved."

"Romantically involved?" I asked.

"Don't look so baffled. Jake and I are spending the night in Worcester. This weekend is supposed to be a romantic getaway."

I shook my head and said, "I'm more baffled by your inviting your brothers along!"

Anna leaned forward and whispered, "Mom, it's a first for us as a couple, and I'm a little nervous."

"That's ridiculous, Anna, because you have nothing to be nervous about. You are both searching for happiness, and I say, seek and you shall find!"

Anna giggled before letting out a deep cleansing breath.

Two days later, Jake picked Anna up at our house on Washington Street. He pulled into the driveway in a green Subaru Forester, and I was secretly glad it wasn't a red pickup truck. I was beginning to like this young man more and more. He was definitely a grownup. After seeing him in action at City Hall, and observing him with Anna for the last few months, I found him to be daring and kind at the same time. And when he rang the doorbell at seven o'clock sharp, I said a prayer for his and Anna's future before I opened the door.

"Good morning, Mrs. Malone."

"What happened to 'Ellie'?" I chuckled.

"You're right," he said. "Let me try that again. Good morning, Ellie!"

I winked. "That's better. We're making progress!"

"Jake, is that you?" Anna called from the top of the stairs.

"Who else would be ringing your doorbell so early on a Saturday morning?" he called back.

"I'm ready!" she said in her highest voice as she started walking down the stairs.

I didn't have to look up to know that she looked amazing because I was staring at Jake's face when he caught his first glimpse.

"You'd better get going," I advised. "It's a long ride to Worcester. Drive carefully and keep your eyes on the road!"

As I handed Anna her purple fleece, I gave her a quick kiss on the cheek and whispered in her ear, "It will be cold by the lake, and purple is the winning color."

"I know, Mom," Anna called over her shoulder as she flew out the door. "Go, Cross, go!"

"Once a cheerleader, always a cheerleader," I called back with a parting wave. I lingered long enough to see Jake open the car door for Anna, and at that exact moment, the sun came out. Everything is possible in the month of May!

* * *

Safely on their way, Anna started talking, and she didn't stop until they pulled into the Kennebunk service plaza on the interstate. Then she plunged in again commenting on the giant statue of a moose.

Jake unbuckled his seat belt and looked at Anna. "How about a cup of coffee?"

"That sounds great, especially if you add a muffin!"

Happy to get out of the car, Anna used the curb to stretch her calf muscles.

"Ah, yes," said Jake, admiring her legs. "I almost forgot how much you like muffins. Would blueberry be okay?"

Anna answered with a grin. "That's my favorite! If you hit the coffee stand, I'll use the ladies'. We're not even halfway there!"

Jake laughed and gave her a snappy salute. "Aye, aye, ma'am! I'll see to it! We'll be back on the road in ten minutes flat!"

They pulled out of the rest stop ten minutes later. "Mission accomplished!" Jake shouted as his foot hit the gas pedal.

As Anna settled into her breakfast, it was Jake who couldn't stop talking. Anna listened in amazement while this usually quiet man told her about working in his father's garage when he was in high school. He told her how his father used to sing while he worked under the hood of expensive sports cars and rusty old beaters, but he only ever sang one song: "Ole Buttermilk Sky," a 1940s favorite by Hoagy Carmichael. As they passed over the bridge into New Hampshire, Jake started to sing:

> *Ole buttermilk sky*
> *I'ma keepin' my eye peeled on you*
> *What's the good word tonight?*
> *Are you gonna be mellow tonight?*
> *Ole buttermilk sky*
> *Can't you see my little donkey and me?*
> *We're as happy as a Christmas tree*
> *Headed for the one I love*
> *I'm gonna pop her the question, that question*

Do you darling, do you do?
It'll be easy, oh, so easy
If I can only bank on you…

First, Anna started to giggle, but as Jake kept singing the hokey-sounding verses over and over again, the giggles grew into laughter, and the laughter turned into tears of pure delight.

"Who are you?" Anna asked in disbelief. "You are by far the strangest person I have ever met!"

Jake interrupted his song just long enough to respond, "Maybe, but I'm also the one you are going to love for the rest of your life."

Anna briefly choked on her coffee and covered with a cough, but Jake's eyes never left the road. She suddenly remembered what her brother Joe had once told her: Men talk more when they're shoulder to shoulder than when they're face to face. True or not, sitting next to Jake was turning out to be a learning experience! And now she was anxious to introduce Jake to her brothers. It would be interesting to see their reaction to her new guy.

CHAPTER 16

2014

Upon arriving at Lake Quinsigamond, Jake and Anna realized they were an hour early, but Joe's Jeep was already there.

When Anna opened the car door, she was hit by a blast of cold air, so she reached back for her fleece on the backseat before stepping out into the big chill. She shivered and playfully said, "You're going to have to wear a jacket, babe."

"Like those Herculean oarsmen out there on the water, I'm leaving my jacket in the car," Jake tossed back. Then he looked up and noticed a man waving at them. "Hey, Anna, who…? I bet it's your brother Joe!"

Anna didn't hear a word he said because she had already returned to the car to grab his jacket. When she finally caught up, she spied Joe and Natalie approaching with their newborn tucked in a baby carrier. She waved and shouted, "Hey, family! How's my little niece doing?"

Within seconds Joe was hugging Anna, Natalie was shaking hands with Jake, and everyone was talking at once.

Anna moved close to Natalie to steal a peek at the baby.

"Ah, Stella Grace Malone, you're a beauty," she said.

Natalie laughed. "I'm not sure you would be that smitten with her if you heard her two a.m. wail."

At this point, Joe had to add his two cents. "Mom and Dad were right when they told us you fall in love with your children, and that makes all the difference. When they're your own, the late-night feedings and dozens of dirty diapers don't really seem that bad."

Now it was Anna's turn to laugh. "Easy for you to say, Dr. Dad. You're a pediatrician!"

Jake enjoyed listening to the family's banter, so he didn't say a word until he found himself standing next to Stella.

"Hi, Stella!" he said as he wiggled her foot. "I like your name."

"Thank you," said Natalie. "It suits her sparkle."

Jake looked up and smiled. "She's perfect! Does she have a namesake?"

Joe was quick to answer. "Yes, my grandmother. She was the daughter of a Yankee sea captain."

"Well, I'm sure she was amazing because she helped to create this little miracle!"

Natalie poked Anna's side with her elbow. "You should keep this one. He's got superb taste, and he's smart!

Joe leaned forward and whispered, "Why not throw in good-looking, too?" And then he leaned back and practically shouted, "So Anna, are you going to introduce us to this new guy of yours?"

Anna tossed Joe a look and grabbed Jake's hand. "Natalie, Joe, this is Jake Summers." Now her eyes were smiling. "And Jake, as you probably guessed, this is my brother Joe and his wife, Natalie."

Jake grinned. "I see the resemblance!"

Everybody laughed, nodded their approval, and shook hands.

"So where is Frank? I thought our brother planned to join us with his blushing bride!"

"Oh, yeah, I was supposed to tell you that Frank has to be at a track meet today." Joe smiled in his typical half-smile way, and then he shook his head and added, "I don't know about you, but I for one have a hard time imagining Frank as the coach instead of the runner."

"I know what you mean. Do you remember how Mom used to stand by the track and shout 'Vaya, vaya, vaya!' to distract the competition? Nine out of ten times, she got the other runners to look! It was a brilliant strategy."

"Yes, it was!" Joe laughed. "Frank is probably using that same tactic today."

"True, but if we don't get to the porch and find a good spot along the railing, we're going to miss today's races!" With that nudge, Anna got everyone moving toward the lake.

As they walked along the path, Joe looked at Jake and casually commented, "Okay, you seem like a nice enough guy, but if you're going to watch the first heat with us, you're going to have to cover up that WPI T-shirt."

"Don't worry, Joe. I've got his jacket right here," quipped Anna as she held up Jake's windbreaker. "I'll make sure he conceals his loyalty to that other team."

Jake buried his hands in his pockets and shrugged. "Actually, I was hoping I could stop by the WPI boathouse and say hello to Coach Harding. I didn't row while I was in college, but I used to hang out at the boathouse fixing things. When Coach found out I had some mad skills with power tools, he practically adopted me."

Joe laughed and nodded. "You should definitely stop in and see your coach. There are at least three qualifying heats, so you have plenty of time before the finals start."

"Well, if that's the case, I'm sticking with the guy who brought me," said Anna. "We'll meet you at Holy Cross's boathouse before the finals begin."

"That's a solid plan, and it gives Natalie and me a chance to introduce Stella to the Holy Cross team."

With that settled, Anna and Jake walked over to WPI's boathouse. Before stepping over the threshold, Jake put his arm around Anna and whispered, "Are you ready to enter the enemy camp?"

"My brothers went to Holy Cross, but I went to NYU, and I'm a Violet for life."

Of course that answer called for another question. "Your mascot was a violet?"

"I know it's not fierce, but NYU students would rather be creative than intimidating. Either way, today I'm with you, and my family seems to be on board with that."

Jake gave her a quick squeeze, and they stepped into the dark, cool boathouse. Coach Harding was standing next to a stack of oars, reviewing the day's schedule. His rowers had already carried their boats to the dock. He looked up as he heard them enter and recognized Jake right away.

"Could that be Jake 'I never smile' Summers? How long has it been?"

"It's been too long! How are you, Coach?"

"I'll be better after today! And who's the lovely lady who is putting a smile on your face?"

Jake grabbed Coach Harding's hand and pumped it hard. "This is Anna Malone of Bath, Maine. She's a gem, but I have to warn you that she has a flaw. Both of her brothers went to Holy Cross, and one of them even rowed for Coach Pugliese."

While the coach put his right hand over his heart, he put his left hand on Anna's shoulder. "Because you're so pretty, I'm going to overlook your affinity for purple oars, but tell me, what's your brother's name, the one who rowed for Pug?"

"Joe Malone. He stroked for the lightweight varsity eight boat that took silver at the NERC about ten years ago."

"I remember that name, and I remember that boat. Of course, we manage to beat them every once in a while."

Coach Harding winked at Anna and grinned like a kid. "I'd like to meet your brother and congratulate him on his achievement. Few men know the sweetness of a varsity eight victory, and he's one of them!"

"Well, I'm sure he'd like that. But tell me, Coach, what was Jake like back in the day?"

Harding leaned toward Anna and with a low, husky voice, whispered, "He was the quiet man on campus. If you could get ten words out of him, it was a big win. Does he talk a lot when he's with you?"

Anna laughed. "This morning he talked nonstop from Bath to Worcester!"

Harding looked over at Jake, paused, and then looked back at Anna. "My dear, if that is true, then you're either a miracle worker or this young man is falling head over heels."

* * *

Jake and Anna were standing shoulder to shoulder on the porch of the Donahue Rowing Center when WPI advanced to the petite finals. A half hour later, Holy Cross's varsity eight boat finished second in its heat and made it to the grand finals, along with Cornell, Trinity, George Washington, Delaware, and Boston University. The porch was overflowing with alumni, parents, rowers, and friends. When the finals were about to begin, Joe yelled, "Go, Cross, go!" but Natalie, still holding Stella in her carrier, remained quiet. When Anna noticed the fatigue on Natalie's face, she nudged Jake.

"Do you think Natalie is going to last another six and a half minutes?"

Jake shook his head. "I'm not sure, but Stella is not going to be happy when this porch erupts with hooting, hollering, and the ringing of cow bells. Maybe I should offer to take Stella inside and rock her a bit in a quieter spot."

"Great idea, but ask Natalie right now because this porch is about to rock!"

Jake walked over to Natalie and within seconds she was undoing her baby carrier and passing her little ten-pound bundle into Jake's strong arms. Anna couldn't hear what she was saying, but the expression on her face spoke volumes. She was clearly relieved and grateful. Anna, however, was surprised by her own feelings when she saw Jake cradle little Stella in his arms. Until that moment she had never seen this tender side of him, and she liked it. On the outside, Jake seemed hardened by his experiences in combat, and sometimes even damaged. But now, as the afternoon sun was beginning to drop, a shaft of light showed a soft expression on his face that touched Anna's heart. With Stella safely nestled in the crook of his arm, he looked up, caught Anna's eye and winked. Anna signaled him back with a thumbs-up and a bright smile. Jake was obviously a man who possessed more than mechanical talents!

At the end of the day, the regatta proved to be a big win for the Malones. Not only did Holy Cross beat Trinity and BU to win a silver medal, but Joe saw his beloved crew team finish less than one seat behind Cornell in a tight race. Jake had clearly passed Joe's litmus test, and Anna was thrilled.

On the ride back to the hotel, Jake asked about Stella's namesake.

"So what can you tell me about the original Stella? If your grandmother was a sea captain's daughter, she must have lived an interesting life."

"Interesting indeed. The whole truth may shock you…So, my grandmother, Stella Rose Donovan, was illegitimate, the love child of a sea captain's daughter and a handsome mariner—"

"Wait, do you mean your great-grandmother was also a sea captain's daughter?"

"What can I say, I have salt water running through my veins."

"Well, that explains a lot!"

Anna laughed. "My great-grandfather, the Yankee captain, fell in love with the daughter of a much older captain, who happened to be his father's best friend."

With his eyes on the road, Jake shook his head. "Wow, men who go to sea really know how to spin a web…"

"And sometimes those webs become scandals, like this one. Our dashing sea captain wasn't free to marry. His wife was alive, and divorce was not an option. She was mentally unstable, so he felt morally bound to stay with her even after Stella Rose was born. Years later, after his wife died, he married my great-grandmother and gave Stella Rose his family name."

Stopped at a red light, Jake looked over at Anna. "That's quite a story! So what was Stella Rose Donovan's maiden name?"

After a long pause, Anna answered. "No one has ever asked, and no one has ever answered that question. I have no idea."

The light turned green. As Jake focused on the road, he asked a follow-up question.

"Was your grandmother born in Bath?"

"No, I think she was born on her mother's family farm east of the Kennebec River, but she later moved to Bath."

For a moment Jake seemed lost in thought, then he said, "Did you know Lake Quinsigamond used to be called Long Pond?"

"No, I didn't know that," Anna answered, slightly confused by this apparently random question.

"Both Long Reach and Long Pond are protected waterways, and that's why they're so valuable."

Anna laughed. "Well, that's good to know, Jake. Thank you for sharing."

"I mean…water seems to be our common denominator. From one generation to the next, water carries us forward…" Jake glanced quickly at Anna and returned his eyes to the road. He finished his thought with, "I have a feeling the tides brought us together, Anna."

She reached over and gently put her hand on Jake's leg.

"I agree."

Jake put his foot on the gas, ignored the yellow light, and blasted through the intersection.

"Whoa!" said Anna. "What's the rush?"

Jake answered with another quick glance and a boyish grin. "If you want me to slow down, you'll have to take your hand off of my leg."

Anna chuckled as she pulled her hand back. "Okay, I'll try to keep my hands to myself for safety's sake, but it won't be easy!"

Jake laughed out loud. "I'm glad it's not easy!"

He came to a full stop at the next red light, glanced out his side window, and stopped talking. He stared blankly at the building across the street. It was the largest Veterans Administration Center in the region, and a group of disheveled veterans were sitting on its front steps having a smoke. They looked like a troop of lost boys.

Sensing a dramatic shift, Anna asked quietly, "Are you still with me?"

"Sorry. I'm here…"

The light turned green. Jake stepped on the gas, drove to the next corner, turned into the hotel's parking lot and pulled into the first available spot. After turning off the car, he looked over at Anna's sweet face and finished his thought.

"But I think I should be there, and I don't know why I'm not. Why am I the guy sitting here with the gorgeous girl when I could be sitting over there or not at all?"

"I don't know the answer. Only God knows. But I don't believe your survival was an accident. Sometimes love wins."

Tears began to fall from Jake's ocean-blue eyes. He let them go, and more followed before he pinched the bridge of his nose and managed to choke back his grief.

"Would you mind if I went over and talked to those guys for a while?"

"I would be disappointed if you didn't. I'll check us in and meet you up in the room."

Jake reached over and kissed her cheek gratefully, then stepped out of the car and walked across the street. The men looked up as Jake approached, and Anna saw one of them stand up and shake his hand. As she entered the hotel, she looked back and saw that the men were talking. She could only imagine what stories they would tell and how those stories would affect Jake.

A half hour later, Jake knocked at the door of their hotel room, and Anna opened it dressed in a white silk shirt that barely covered the fact that she wasn't wearing anything else. Jake's eyes traveled up and down her body, and his devilish grin said he approved. Anna pulled him into the room. Without a word, she unfastened his belt, unzipped his pants, and pressed her mouth over his. When she finally released him, she whispered an answer to his earlier question. "Jake, you survived so you could save me. You've rescued me from a dark place where only broken hearts go. Now it's my turn to show you how important your life is to me."

Jake leaned toward Anna until their noses touched, and then he pulled her even closer until night turned into morning.

CHAPTER 17

1887

When *El Capitan* sailed into the South Street Seaport on the lower east side of Manhattan on a cold February afternoon in 1887, Sarah was waiting on the dock with Lily at her side. Both mother and child were dressed in dark-blue coats that allowed the bottoms of their softly draped skirts to show. Sarah's coat, trimmed with a black velvet collar, hugged her bodice but flared slightly from the waist to mid-calf. Lily's coat was loose-fitting so that she could twist and wiggle at will. Her stylish red hat matched her mother's perfectly. It was adorned with a blue feather and tied under her chin with a black satin ribbon. Lily was only three years old, and her hair refused to stay tucked inside the wide rim of her new hat. Her golden locks dancing in the wind, she looked like an angel with a runaway halo. Her small hands were encased in soft blue mittens, and Sarah was holding onto her left hand extra tight. Everyone who passed by complimented her pretty coat and her glorious hat, and Lily said thank you by waving her hand like a little princess.

As soon as Thomas stepped out of his cabin and looked toward the dock, he spotted Sarah and Lily. He waved his hand high above his head, and they waved back euphorically. Sarah lifted Lily up so she could have a better view of her father on the quarterdeck of his ship, and Lily giggled with joy.

"There's your papa, Lily! He's back! In a few days, we're going to take the train home to Bath, and then Papa will be able to tuck you in every night!"

Sarah gave the child a hug and gently set her down again.

Ten minutes later, Thomas rushed down the gang-plank and embraced his pretty young wife. After a long hello kiss, Thomas knelt down in front of his daughter.

"Why Lily, you've grown like a weed." He pulled her close to him, took her hand in his, and placed it over his heart.

"Do you feel my heart beating?" he asked.

With a twinkle in her eye, Lily nodded yes.

"It's been beating for you all this time that we've been apart."

Feeling the beat of his heart and hearing his warm, steady voice, Lily leaned in and softly kissed her father's bearded face.

For a moment, Sarah thought she saw tears in Thomas's eyes, but he squeezed the bridge of his nose and seemed to will them away. Still holding Lily's hand, he stood up and wrapped his free hand around Sarah's neck. He pulled her close, and she let him cover her mouth with his. When she finally stepped back to speak, his wet kiss still lingered on her lips.

"Next time we are going with you," she said.

Thomas grinned. "Yes, yes you are, and it won't be on the *El Capitan*. In two months, we set sail on the *Paul Revere*."

Sarah squealed with delight. "Oh, that's wonderful news!"

"You will love it, Sarah, and I think you will find the living quarters quite comfortable. They may not be palatial, but the space is more than adequate for a family of three."

Sarah couldn't resist the urge to tease her captain. She looked away and coyly said, "Maybe during the voyage we can make that number four."

Hearing that wish, Thomas reached down and picked up his sweet little Lily.

"Let's get home to Bath as soon as possible so we can plan our voyage, a voyage that will take us around Cape Horn, up to San Francisco, and across the Pacific to Yokohama, Japan." His lips tickled her ear as he whispered, "I want to show my girls the world."

"Whoa," said Sarah with a giggle as contagious as Lily's. "You've just stepped foot on land. The company's carriage is waiting around the corner to take us to your father's apartment. How does a hot bath sound?"

"It sounds like a dream, especially if you throw in a warm towel followed by a brandy and a few hours under the covers with you!"

"Now that would be heavenly, but Lily may have other plans."

"That's all right. I'm happy just being near you."

When they arrived at the carriage, Thomas told the driver there was no need to hurry and asked him to take the scenic route along the banks of the East River so he could get a good look at the Brooklyn Bridge. As Sarah stepped into the carriage, she sensed her husband's excitement. It was both a relief and a joy to be together again. Thomas lifted Lily up as if she were a feather and gently placed her next to Sarah, then he climbed in beside them to ride through the city and enjoy its dazzling views.

On their way to Brooklyn Heights, they spied a stunning ship sailing up the river, and their conversation naturally turned to the family business. Thomas was anxious to discuss all the news that Sarah had mentioned in her letters. Henry had transitioned from being an owner of his shipbuilding company to being a board member of the New England Shipbuilding Company. According to

Sarah, he was adapting well to his new position, and he was choosing to be happy.

"I'm sorry your father was called back to Bath. He wanted to be here when you arrived, but there was an emergency at Long Reach. Seriously, Thomas, your father has been working around the clock to promote the company's new two-thousand-ton ship, the *Francis*, which, if all goes well, should be ready to leave the ways next October. I wish I had his fighting spirit. He's truly amazing. "

"Oh, I know. I spent most of my youth trying to be just like him, but now I know how foolish that was. He's one of a kind!"

"Well, he admires you, too. He asked me to congratulate you on a successful voyage, and he wanted me to tell you that you are the best-looking Captain Goss!"

Thomas threw back his head and laughed. "That sounds like something my father would say!"

"Of course, he also had a request. He would like you to stop at a few of the shipyards in Boston on our way back to Bath. He wants you to promote the *Francis*. He's excited about its sale."

A tiny nerve twitched beneath Thomas's eye and his jaw tightened. He understood his father's excitement. The *Francis* was a significant accomplishment for the newly formed New England Shipbuilding Company, but more importantly, it was named in honor of his brother. "How are things really going at home?"

"I think your father would tell you that shipbuilding is changing and so is Long Reach. But I doubt there's anything the Goss family can do to stop that change. It's time to regroup and fill up our souls at a family dinner. Tomorrow the sun will shine, and the sky will be bluer than it is today. Just wait and see."

The horses came to a sudden stop in front of a stately two-story brownstone. Thomas stepped out of the carriage with Lily in his arms and turned to help Sarah. They walked up the granite steps to a dark mahogany door with beveled glass, and as Thomas watched Sarah turn the key, he whispered almost reverently, "Did I tell you how much I've missed you?"

"No, but tonight you can tell me as many times as you like."

* * *

Two days later, Sarah and Thomas boarded a train for Boston with their darling Lily in tow. As the porter helped them get settled in their first-class seats, several passengers sitting nearby took notice.

"Has anyone ever mistaken you for British royalty?" asked a distinguished gentleman with a shock of gray hair and a stylish mustache.

Thomas shook his head. "No, not ever. We're from Bath, Maine, not England."

"Ah, yes, I can tell from your accent, but your grand sense of style suggests some place grander than the shipyards of Long Reach."

"You know Bath?" asked Thomas, surprised.

"Of course I know Bath! I'm a news correspondent for the *New York Times*, and I've spent the last fifteen years covering the shipping industry in Bristol, Liverpool, London, New York, Philadelphia, San Francisco, and Hong Kong. Bath's sailing ships are recognized around the world. But don't worry. I'm not on assignment right now, as my father's health is poor, and I'm on my way to Concord to visit him and my mother. I've been away too long. I'm afraid I haven't been the best son."

Thomas sighed. "I can appreciate that kind of guilt. Shipmasters and news correspondents seem to have a lot in common, especially when it comes to time away from home. If I could spend more time on land than at sea, I think I could help my father save his business."

"Forgive me for asking—I am a reporter, after all— what is your father's business?"

"He is a master shipbuilder. He was co-owner of

Goss and Sawyer. Now he is on the board of a newly formed company, the New England Shipbuilding Company, and he is their chief solicitor in New York City. Unfortunately, business has been slow lately."

Hearing sadness creep into her husband's voice, Sarah grabbed Thomas's hand and leaned forward to add a bit of levity to the darkening conversation.

"Don't get my husband started on the shipping industry. You won't be able to cork his passion! By the way, I'm Mrs. Goss, and you may call me Sarah."

The handsome stranger laughed. "I would never disagree with such a lovely lady! My name is Walter Hudson, and now it's your turn."

Thomas reached out to shake Walter's hand. "I'm Captain Thomas Goss, and this outspoken beauty is my wife, Sarah Gannett Goss."

For a moment, Walter remained silent, then he asked, "Do you mean 'Gannett,' as in Arthur Gannett and Company?"

Sarah answered, "Yes, Arthur Gannett is my uncle. I suppose you've heard of him."

Now Walter laughed without restraint. "Yes, Mrs. Goss, I've heard of the maritime prince. Ironically, I was right from the start. You *are* a royal family!"

Appreciating the irony, Thomas chided, "As a mere Goss, I don't feel royal, but Sarah Gannett Goss is a different story. But don't be fooled by the red coat and the fashionable white hat. At home I call her Sadie!"

Walter looked surprised. "I thought the Gannetts came from English stock. Is there a little French in the family bloodlines as well?"

Sarah blushed. "My great-grandmother's name was Elise Caron. Her family settled in Wiscasset in 1765. If one believes the family stories, a dashing sea captain from Bath docked his ship in the harbor one day, and two weeks later they were married."

"And who would that captain be, Mrs. Goss?"

"That captain would be Joseph Gannett, and the fruit of that union would be a fleet of magnificent sailing ships."

Walter Hudson, the hard-nosed reporter, nodded in agreement. "Your family saga is worthy of telling. It's better than fiction!"

Sarah laughed out loud. "Are you suggesting you would like the byline, Mr. Hudson?"

Just as Walter was about to say yes, the train lurched, and Lily, who had fallen asleep on her father's lap, woke with a start and began to cry. She reached for her mother, and Thomas willingly handed her over to Sarah's waiting arms. With his hands and lap now free, Thomas seized the moment to stand up and stretch his long, lean frame.

"Walter, would you like to walk to the dining car with me? I can assure you my wife is not about to share her family's secrets with you, but I, on the other hand, love to tell stories when someone else is buying the drinks!"

Sarah raised an eyebrow. "Mr. Hudson, don't believe a word he says, but when I'm ready to tell the tale, I'll remember you."

"I've enjoyed our chat, and I would be honored to help you write that history. Whether you resemble the Carons or the Gannetts, you are breathtakingly beautiful."

"Thank you, Mr. Hudson. You're too kind, but if you really want to touch my heart, have a drink with my husband and help him relax."

"My pleasure, madam." And with a smile and a slight bow, Walter Hudson followed Thomas to the bar.

A few hours later, the train pulled into Boston's Union Station. The New England Shipbuilding Company had arranged for a carriage to meet them, and within minutes they were unpacking at a cozy inn that was just a block or two away from the house where Paul Revere had once lived. Thomas was well aware of the North End's rich history, and he was glad that his father had asked him to stay in Boston. It gave him a chance to walk along the cobbled streets where liberty was born.

The tall Yankee sea captain and his family spent three whole days in Boston, and every evening, they walked down the street where Paul Revere had lived, stopping in front of Revere's colonial home, where Thomas would say, "It's hard to believe that I will soon command the *Paul Revere* and in so doing enter the pages of history. Please God, let me bring honor to her name because she bears the name of a true son of liberty."

In reply, Sarah would grab Thomas's hand, stand on the tips of her toes, and kiss his bearded cheek with tender lips and an adoring heart. "You're my hero, Thomas."

"But I'm no Paul Revere. Marrying you, Sarah, was the best decision I ever made. You're my greatest victory!"

They laughed and continued walking down the cobblestone street swinging Lily between them.

When the happy trio arrived in Bath later that week, Captain Henry Goss was waiting at the station, and he greeted each of them with a bear hug, starting with his little flower, Lily, moving on to Sarah, and finally embracing his son. Thomas hugged him back for as long as he could, and then he reluctantly let go. He looked intently at his father's weathered face and noticed how much his father had aged while he was away at sea; however, his father's smile was still warmer than sunshine, his voice was strong, and in his arms a moment ago, Thomas knew he was home.

CHAPTER 18

2014

I t was Saturday night, and that meant Anna was at the Moonlight Cinema in Brunswick. Just a few weeks after arriving in Maine, she had discovered this small, locally owned theater for indie and cutting-edge films, and she became a regular. Tonight's showing was a new release, *Begin Again*, and she had convinced Jake to go with her. She also convinced him to sit up front in one of the comfy couches. They shared a bucket of popcorn as they enjoyed the romantic chemistry of Keira Knightley and Mark Ruffalo on screen. Jake pressed his knee against Anna's thigh the entire time, and they were happy as clams.

When the movie ended and the credits rolled, Anna whispered, "I hope they cast Mark Ruffalo as the Tacoma police detective when they turn my screenplay into a motion picture."

"Is that happening?" Jake looked surprised. "I mean, you talked about your setting and characters last week at the beach, but I had no idea you were this close to the finish line."

Anna stood up with a burst of nervous energy. "Let's get some gelato, and I'll tell you all about it."

Once they were outside and strolling down the street, Anna grabbed Jake's hand.

"You know I've been writing every day for months. Well, Doris introduced me to her friend, a VP of Development at Coastline Studios, when she was here for a visit, and I pitched her my story in Doris's kitchen. She shared my summary with Coastline's president, and now he wants to talk about it."

"Well, if you have Doris Van der Waag in your corner, you'll go ten rounds and win."

Anna laughed. "It's possible!"

They were standing in front of the gelato shop, and Jake was about to open the door when Anna continued.

"Doris set up a conference call for tomorrow morning at ten."

Jake didn't move.

"What's wrong, Jake?"

"I'm happy for you Anna, but I'm worried this movie deal will take you away, and I think you belong here."

* * *

The next day Anna walked over to Doris's stunning Italianate home and rang the bell. While she waited, she admired the door's rich, hand-carved wood and smiled. This was one of the prettiest houses in Bath, and just looking at it made her feel happy. Suddenly, the door opened, and Doris welcomed her.

"Good morning, sunshine! I'm glad you're early. I've got coffee and scones waiting in the kitchen!"

Anna laughed. "Thank you! Like my mom, I need coffee! And a scone would be nice."

"Well, come on in, and let's get started! We have to strategize a little before we place this call."

Minutes later, Anna was listening to the voice of Warren Dunlap, the president of Coastline Studios, on speakerphone.

"Ms. Malone, we love your screenplay! And if you agree to work with us, we can make it a great movie. We'd like to green-light this project."

Doris jumped up and did her happy dance while Anna closed her eyes and jumped back into the business of making movies.

"Wonderful! Let's talk contract! I want to have final approval on any creative changes with the screenplay."

Dunlap readily agreed. "Of course; that's not a problem."

"And I want to be executive producer on the movie."

After a brief pause, Dunlap cleared his throat and gently disagreed. "I was thinking associate producer."

Anna's response was firm and immediate. "This is not my first time at the rodeo, Mr. Dunlap. I'm ready to be an executive producer, and that's not negotiable."

In the short silence that followed, Anna tried to imagine Warren Dunlap, the Hollywood deal-maker, leaning back in his chair three thousand miles away, contemplating his response. And when it came, it was exactly what she had hoped for and expected: "You drive a hard bargain, Anna, but you also know how to tell a great story, so welcome aboard! You're hired as an executive producer!"

CHAPTER 19

2014

The phone rang, and I woke up with a start. I still wasn't used to sleeping alone. Ty had gone back to Baltimore, and I had spent the night tossing and turning. When I reached for my cell phone, I saw the time. It was already nine o'clock. I stood up and tried to bring the room into focus. Freckles, on the other hand, stretched her long dachshund body on the rug and quickly decided to lie down again as if to say, *What's the rush?* I shook my head and wondered how Freckles, my best morning friend, could let me sleep until nine o'clock when usually we were up at six. Obviously, today was not going to be a typical day in Bath!

My sleepy voice croaked "Good morning" into the phone, and a man's voice whispered back.

"Did I wake you, Ellie?"

"Yes, as a matter of fact, you did. Who is this?"

"I'm sorry to be calling so early. It's Bill Marston."

"Oh, Bill, I didn't recognize your rise-and-shine voice. And to what do I owe this wake-up call?"

"Well, I've got good news. The City Council is ready to finalize the timetable for the completion of the Sagadahoc County Memorial Garden. Could you come over to City Hall and look at the calendar with me?"

"Sure, I can do that, but why the urgency?"

"Well, that's the best part. On behalf of Bath's City Council, I would like to offer you a job. We would like you to be the executive director of our newly formed not-for-profit entity, the Sagadahoc Old Cemeteries Association. How does that sound?"

Words failed me for a moment.

"Ellie, are you still there?"

"Yes, I'm here. I'm just stunned. This is the first I've heard of any plan to form a group dedicated to preserving Sagadahoc County's old cemeteries. We should definitely talk about this, but not at City Hall. It's too formal. Save me a seat at the Blue Scone. I'll be there at ten."

And with that decision made, Freckles and I rushed downstairs and out the side door for a quick walk before I jumped into the shower to get ready for what had just become an important summer day.

At ten o'clock sharp, a little bell jingled as I opened the café's French-blue door and greeted Nick and his merry band of servers. As usual, Nick was standing in front of the grill, ready to engage in another battle of words.

"Well, if it isn't the stormy Ellie. Are you here to plot another campaign to save the sacred burial grounds of Maine?"

"No, I'm just meeting a friend and ordering a cup of coffee with a raspberry white chocolate scone."

"Ah, yes, the usual! I think we can handle that. If your friend is the chair of the City Council, he's over at the corner table."

"Thanks, Nick. I do need my comfort food! And for the record, Bill is a friend of mine. There's no conspiracy going on here...at least not today."

Nick smirked, and in that moment he reminded me

of John Belushi in *The Blues Brothers*.

"If you say so, Ellie. It's just another morning in the City of Ships!"

I grabbed my bright-yellow mug and filled it to the brim with dark French roast and proceeded to the back of the restaurant where Bill was waiting with a large gold envelope resting on the table in front of him.

"Hi, Ellie, good to see you. Thanks for coming on such short notice."

"When the chair of the City Council calls, I come running! You've got my undivided attention. What's in the envelope?"

"That's what I like about you, Ellie. You get right to the point."

Bill handed me the official documents, and I perused them as he began to explain the mission.

"This is a list of the forty-eight graves that were exhumed by DOT in order to widen Beacon Street. The remains were cremated, placed in urns, and labeled. When we officially open the garden, the City Council would like you to preside over a ribbon-cutting ceremony and spread the ashes among the newly planted flowers, bushes, and trees."

"Okay, let's look at the calendar and find a reasonable target date. Where are we with construction of the fountain and the statue of a sea captain at the helm? That's my greatest concern because it's the focal point of the garden."

Bill nodded. "The sculptor is confident he will have the work completed in twelve weeks."

"Now I'm excited!" I said as I added some cream to my coffee.

"You're always excited," Bill chuckled. "But I must admit, it's your can-do spirit that has made the Memorial Garden possible. I hope you'll accept the City Council's offer and become the first executive director of SOCA."

I was flattered and speechless. I knew that the State of Maine had formed the Maine Old Cemetery Association in 1968 to begin locating historic cemeteries throughout the state, but I had no idea that MOCA would be willing to help Bath establish its own association to maintain the Memorial Garden as well as the other historic cemeteries in and around the city. This was a victory, and I wanted to call Doris and shout for joy, but first I had to consider the offer on the table. The City of Bath's Department of Cemeteries and Parks is responsible for maintaining 208 acres, and most of that acreage is used for cemeteries. The foreman had told me that during the summer, they have to mow on a three-day cycle, and they do it on a shoestring budget. Without a doubt, SOCA would be a godsend. My answer was crystal clear.

"I accept! And I have lots of ideas to share, like an educational center at the Memorial Garden. We can invite students from the local schools, sponsor lecture series, show films, and we can raise the necessary funds to maintain our cemeteries as they should be."

Bill Marston leaned his chair to the tipping point and laughed like a boy at play. "Ellie, you crack me up, and your enthusiasm is contagious. On behalf of the City of Bath and Sagadahoc County, I officially hire you! Welcome aboard, Madam Director!"

On that triumphant note, we both stood up, and Bill shook my hand and told me to call him as soon as I had decided on a date in 2015 for the Memorial Garden's grand opening. I hurried home to share the good news with Anna. It was almost eleven o'clock, so I presumed she would be awake, but ten years of working in the arts had turned her into the quintessential night owl. Eleven was her seven! When I entered the kitchen, I was surprised to find a note on the counter.

Mom,

Jake stopped by, and we decided to walk up to the Farmers' Market. We left Freckles behind because she only has eyes for you! If you get back before noon, join us. Hasta luego!

Anna XO

* * *

It was a glorious Saturday morning, so naturally the brick path around Waterfront Park was overflowing with friendly people. No one seemed to mind standing in line at the Farmers' Market for flowers, French baguettes, green beans, raspberry tarts, and blueberries. Neighbors and visitors gathered to chat and support their local growers. Jake was patiently waiting in line at the Big Barn Coffee stand, but his eyes were on Anna. She was sitting on a bench near the river and the sun was lighting up her chestnut hair in a luscious way.

A rough voice interrupted his thoughts. "That will be four dollars, sir."

"Right, here you go. Thanks."

Jake grabbed the cups and felt their heat through the cardboard sleeves. He didn't even need to taste the coffee. He breathed in the addictive scent and felt fully awake. The next stop was the flower stand. He set the two cups down on Linda's metal folding table, which was set up behind her white van, and started to examine the Gerber daisies. Linda, one of the friendliest flower vendors in Maine, noticed that Jake was unusually nervous for a Saturday at the market.

"Can I help you?"

Without taking his eyes off the buckets of freshly cut flowers, Jake muttered, "I'm looking for the prettiest daisy you have."

Linda laughed. "They all look pretty this morning, but let me find you a good one." She chose a tall pink Gerber daisy and presented it for Jake's approval.

"That's a good one. I'll take it; thanks." Jake reached in his pocket and pulled out a few dollars.

"Just one dollar," Linda said with a smile.

"Thanks again."

As he turned to leave, Linda picked up the two cups of coffee and said, "Aren't you forgetting something?"

He chuckled, "I think I'm forgetting my brain.

Thank you. I need that coffee!"

Walking toward the river, Jake passed a group of bluesy musicians. He thought the guitarist and drummer were phenomenal, so he raised the daisy in his right hand to salute them. The singer noticed and nodded. Jake was beginning to feel lucky, but as he approached Anna, he slowed down. She was gazing up at the Sagadahoc Bridge, and she looked breathtakingly beautiful in her tight blue jeans and light-green sweater. When she turned around, Jake immediately handed her a cup of coffee.

"Why, Jake, thank you! This coffee smells divine. And I bet that daisy you're holding smells good, too."

"It's for you," he stammered.

As soon as Anna reached for the flower, Jake went down on one knee, and Anna spied a small pouch pressed against the stem of her pink Gerber daisy.

"What's this?" Anna asked with a slight quiver in her voice.

Jake opened his mouth, but he couldn't form a single word.

Anna set her coffee down on the ground, looked inside the pouch, and gasped, "It's a diamond."

Jake found his courage. "I chose a solitaire because you're my one and only. Anna, you know I believe in fate, and I believe that the tides have brought us together for a reason. We are better together than apart. I love you, Anna, and I'm going to pop that question. Will you marry me?"

For Jake, the Farmers' Market disappeared. He didn't notice that people were watching. After a deafening pause, he heard the rush of Anna's voice like a waterfall.

"I love you, Jake. I love you more every day, but let's not hurry."

Anna's words crashed against him and rang in his ears until he couldn't hear anything at all. He stood up and started to walk away, but Anna reached out and grabbed his hand. The circle of onlookers started to disperse.

"Please, Jake, let me explain. Let's sit and talk.

There's a reason I can't say yes right now."

With a stone-cold face, Jake said, "Pick a bench and tell me."

Still holding her pink daisy, Anna sat down on a bench near the dock, and Jake sat down beside her. As she struggled to find the right words, Jake fixed his eyes on the Kennebec.

"Remember the conference call I told you about?"

"Yes."

"Well, Coastline Studios wants to turn my screenplay into a motion picture, and they've agreed to let me produce. It's a dream come true. If I don't seize this opportunity, Jake, it may never come again."

Jake looked up at the clear blue sky and quietly said, "I don't want to take you away from your dream, Anna, but I wish your dream was with me."

He stood up and moved closer to the water, and Anna followed.

"Oh, Jake, you're more than a dream. You're the hot-blooded man I want to go to bed with every night and wake up with every morning."

Jake ran his fingers through his hair and said gruffly, "Then why are you saying no to me?"

Anna came up behind him, wrapped her arms around him, and said, "We'll be shooting on location in Tacoma for at least three months—"

"Three months is nothing!" Jake fired back. "I'm a marine! I can survive a three-month separation! I'm telling you I want to spend the rest of my life with you!"

"Please try to understand. I've been given a chance to produce my own movie, and I have to take it. In the past, I sidelined my art for a guy, and that didn't end well. This project will demand my undivided attention, and I won't be available for a year or more. That's not the way I want our story to begin."

Defeated, Jake bowed his head. "I see. You'll be too busy for us."

With her cheek pressed against his back, Anna pleaded her case. "When I say yes to you, I want to be consumed by you and only you. Will you wait for me, Jake?"

He turned around and faced her. "I'll try," he said. "For right now, I'll give you the time and space you seem to need." He bent down and gently kissed her goodbye.

Anna blinked back tears as she watched him walk away.

* * *

I was sitting in the sunroom, reading the newspaper, when I heard the door open and close. I looked up to see Anna's tear-stained face.

"Where's Jake?"

She began to sob. "He's gone."

I stood up, wrapped my arms around her, and let her cry.

CHAPTER 20

1887

In April, just two months after arriving home, Thomas was packing again, but this time he was packing for three. Making a voyage to Japan with his wife and daughter on the *Paul Revere* would be a dream compared to sailing on the spartan decks of *El Capitan*. Nevertheless, leaving Bath was hard. Fond memories filled all the rooms of his parents' stately colonial home. Whenever his ship dropped anchor in a nearby port, he always returned to Bath to restore his soul in his old second-floor bedroom, which he had once shared with his brothers but now shared with his wife. That once chaotic boyish room was now imbued with soft colors, sweet smells, handmade quilts, and tall windows covered with lace curtains. It had become the private sanctuary of Mr. and Mrs. Thomas Goss. Their daughter, Lily, was sleeping just a few steps down the hallway in the room that had welcomed Thomas's grandmother, Hannah Riggs.

For the still youthful captain, Bath was a safe haven. In his heart of hearts, he never wanted to leave, but his father had taught him that a sea captain was only truly home when he was aboard his ship. Thomas knew that he couldn't stay too long in a comfortable house on a pretty street surrounded by friendly neighbors. For better or worse, that was not part of his life's journey. As a boy, he had dreamed of sailing around the Horn in tall ships. Now, at the seasoned age of thirty-two, he commanded more than twenty men who typically behaved more like hardened criminals than trustworthy sailors, and he sometimes wondered if he was losing his soul. He had tied a sailor's knot, and he was determined to keep his promises, but it was getting harder to find his true north. His silent prayer was that Sarah's presence aboard ship would help him stay the course.

Deep in thought, Thomas was unaware that Sarah had entered the room. She was carrying a laundry basket filled with woolen socks, flannel shirts, and long underwear. Gazing at her husband's handsome profile, she decided to let her playful voice shatter his grownup time.

"Don't close that trunk!"

Thomas jumped. "I didn't hear you come up the stairs. Were you trying to surprise me or frighten me?"

"Why, Thomas, I always like to surprise you," said Sarah as she put the basket down on the bed. "Don't be cross. I come with clean, warm clothes for our return passage. You've often said that in winter the North Atlantic can be freezing and treacherous from Cape Hatteras to New York City. Well, if we're on schedule, we'll be sailing home in February. It may be nice and warm now, but thinking ahead, we need to pack for frigid temperatures as well."

"That's my girl. You're already thinking about the passage home, and we haven't even left Bath. Are you sure you're ready for this?" Thomas asked with a smile.

"If you're not daring enough to leave home, you'll never experience the thrill of a homecoming. Besides, I'd follow my Captain Goss to the ends of the earth!" Sarah answered with her hand touching her heart.

Thomas's brown eyes crinkled as he laughed. "My dear, I'm glad you said that, because that's exactly where we're going."

"Now who is trying to scare whom? Let's not forget we met and fell in love at sea, but I haven't lived aboard ship in quite some time, and this will be Lily's first voyage. I'm definitely anxious, but I am not afraid. I'll miss this house, and I'll miss quilting with your mother and gardening with my sister. But Thomas, Lily and I belong with you."

Thomas took Sarah in his arms and pressed his face into her silky blond hair. "And I belong with you. I'm just worried that this voyage will be long and dangerous. Fortunately, the captain's quarters on the *Paul Revere* are far more luxurious than any cabin on your Uncle Arthur's square-riggers, but it's still not a house on the prettiest street in Bath."

"That's why our homecoming will be so sweet!" said Sarah as she kissed Thomas's chest and then lifted her face to meet his warm lips.

* * *

Two weeks later, Captain Thomas Goss stood on the quarterdeck of the *Paul Revere* in New York City's busy harbor and gave the order to haul anchor. Charlotte and Henry Goss were looking up from the dock below. They were waving and smiling at their darling granddaughter who was blowing kisses while Charlotte shouted, "Goodbye!" Throughout this emotional send-off, Thomas stood tall and silent.

When the ship was under way, he escorted his wife and daughter to their cabin. On the way, they passed Stephen Harris, the first mate, who was furiously cursing at an old sailor with a big belly and an ugly scar that ran from the corner of his eye to the corner of his mouth. Thomas reached for Lily's hand and encouraged her to walk faster, but she had just spied the ship's cat and naturally wanted to follow it. Vowing to punish Stephen for his foul language, Thomas picked Lily up in his arms and carried her the rest of the way.

"Papa, what's the cat's name?" Lily whispered.

"It seems odd, but I don't think she has a name. I've heard the sailors call her the Liverpool cat because that's where they found her. I've also heard some rumor about two kittens without names. Perhaps they have all been waiting for you."

"Oh, Papa, I will name them as soon as I meet them!"

For the first time all day, Thomas smiled. "Lily, I'm glad you're here. My crew and I need you."

From behind, Sarah witnessed the tender moment and sighed. She knew the voyage would be challenging, but she believed their love would sustain them. Besides, the first passage was short and easy. Before rounding Cape Horn, they would dock in Baltimore to load coal destined for San Francisco. The passage from Baltimore to San Francisco would be much longer, but Sarah had packed lots of good books, her violin, beautiful fabric for quilting and sewing, and Lily's favorite toys, including her cloth doll, Annie. As soon as they arrived in their ma-hogany-paneled cabin, she began to unpack their treasure chest and she reunited Lily with Annie.

"Lily, I think it's time for you and Annie to take a nap."

Sarah put her hand on the glass knob and opened the door to Lily's adjoining room with as much ceremo-ny as the launching of a ship. She wanted Lily to view her room as if it were a secret garden aboard ship, and the magic worked. Lily's eyes opened wide and fell on a sleigh bed made of pumpkin pine, just like the floors of her grandparents' house. The bed's downy mattress was covered with a large patchwork quilt, blue and white, just like the colors of DeGroote and Peck's flag, which flew high over the deck of the *Paul Revere*. Lily jumped into her inviting bed, and within minutes she was asleep and dreaming of a few lost kittens and their mother.

* * *

After departing Baltimore, the *Paul Revere* enjoyed fair winds and following seas, and Lily met four new friends: the Liverpool cat, a white kitten, a black kitten, and a sixteen-year-old cabin boy named Toby, who had red hair and big ears. On a sunny afternoon, the five fast friends could usually be found lounging on the starboard deck. As cabin boy, Toby was assigned the important duty of protecting Lily from misfortune. The captain had commanded him to accompany Lily wherever she wanted to go, and Lily always wanted to go in search of the Liverpool cat and her kittens. Since Toby was the oldest of twelve, seven of whom were girls, he knew how to drag out a game and capture a child's imagination. Lily and Toby played hide and seek with the cats for well over a month before discovering their secret spot at the center of a large coil of rope in the bow of the ship. Keeping her promise, Lily named the Liverpool cat Molly as soon as she met her, and she named the white and black kittens Moby and Midnight. It was love at first sight!

When the *Paul Revere* passed over the equator, her raucous crew uncorked the rum they had been saving and started to drink. A few hours later, they started to haze the new sailors in cruel and creative ways. Thomas knew it would be a frightening day and a horrible night for Sarah and Lily to witness, so he insisted that they remain in their cabin until the rowdy behavior ended. Lily was not happy and cried and whined all day long.

"Where is Toby? Isn't he going to play with me today?" she asked her father with a pout.

Thomas shook his head. "I'm sorry, Lily, but Toby isn't feeling well today. He's resting in his bunk. He'll be up and about tomorrow. Don't worry."

But Lily did worry. Toby had told her once that they were soul mates, and that was even better than being shipmates. Lily believed him. In fact, she believed everything Toby told her. He was her best friend, and if he were sick, she would have to help take care of him. Lily was almost four years old and mature beyond her years, but she was definitely not old enough to wander around the ship looking for Toby's sleeping quarters. Of course, she was also too young to know that, so when she was supposed to be napping, she slipped out of her cabin to find Toby. She passed the ship's wheel and heard a sailor singing loudly, and then she climbed down the ladder to the lower deck like one of the kittens.

Suddenly, she heard a crash behind her and turned to see a dirty, smelly sailor sprawled out on the ship's wet floor. Her mouth opened, and she was about to scream when two long arms scooped her up. It was Toby, red-faced and sweating. He tried to run with Lily in his arms, but her dangling leg hit something sharp, and she screamed in pain. Toby stopped and saw that a red stain was growing on Lily's white bloomers. He caught a glimpse of a rusty nail, and knew instantly that Lily was in trouble, so instead of taking her back to her cabin, he carried her directly to Giovanni's workroom.

Giovanni was considerably older than most of the crew. He found no pleasure in hazing new sailors, but he was willing to pierce their ears. If they were sober, he would also give them tattoos. He strongly believed that a sailor should be clear-headed when he chose a permanent tattoo for a particular part of his body. Waking up with a vulgar image or word on your arm, buttocks, or chest was not the beginning of a good day. Therefore, as the crew performed their equatorial rituals and drank themselves to unconsciousness, Giovanni retreated to his workroom below deck. As the ship's carpenter, Giovanni was one of the most important members of the crew. In addition to his expert skills with a hammer and a saw, he was revered for his ability to heal most shipboard ailments and injuries. Toby, like most of the sailors aboard ship, called him Doc.

"Doc, can you help Lily? She's bleeding."

Startled, Giovanni looked up from his workbench. "Santa María! What happened? Put her down! Let me take a look."

Toby quickly obeyed. Lily was sobbing, but in between sobs, she tried to talk.

"I was looking for Toby." She took a breath. "Papa said he was sick." Her next words were lost as she buried her face in Toby's chest. She was seated on Giovanni's workbench, but she was still holding onto Toby.

"Okay, sweet Lily, let me take a look," said Giovanni as softly as he could.

When he saw the gash, he turned to Toby and asked him to grab the bottle of whiskey on the nearby shelf.

"Whiskey? With no disrespect, Doc, but don't you think she's a bit young?"

"Don't be a fool! I'm going to clean the wound. Grab some of those washcloths, too!"

"Of course! I can do that."

Lily's leg was now drenched in blood. The gash was long and jagged. When Toby stepped back and looked directly at it, he felt weak in the knees, but he focused on Giovanni's instructions. Spinning around, he grabbed the whiskey with his left hand and the stack of neatly folded cloths with his right hand. In a smooth handoff, he passed the whiskey to Giovanni, and then he heard Lily scream.

"This will only sting for a moment, little sailor girl," said Giovanni in a calm, steady voice, but Lily didn't hear a word. She was trying hard to get away from the burning-hot liquid.

Toby jumped up to sit beside her on the bench, and he put his arm around her shoulders. "Hush now, Lily, don't cry. Doc is just washing your cut so it doesn't get infected. A rusty old nail scraped your leg, but Doc is going to make it better, and I'm going to pound that nail hard with a hammer, so it will never hurt you again!"

Lily stopped screaming. Giovanni gently wiped her tears away with one of the remaining cloths. When he glanced over at Toby, he saw that the boy was wiping his own eyes with the back of his shirtsleeve. Maybe the rumors aboard ship were true. Toby, the cabin boy, was Lily's guardian angel. True or not, the old carpenter knew that Toby had saved Lily from a potentially deadly infection.

"Please don't tell Papa," Lily said with a sniffle.

"We have to tell your papa," said Giovanni. He's the captain. He's in charge of everyone, especially you."

"He won't let me play with Toby, or look for the kittens. Oh, *please* don't tell him!"

"I have an idea. The three of us will tell your papa together, and we'll tell him that you have to come to my workroom every day for a week so I can change your bandage and make sure your wound is healing properly. Your father will understand, and he will let you visit me."

Lily nodded in agreement. And from that day forward, Toby, Lily, and Giovanni would call themselves the three pirates of the *Paul Revere*. When Toby and Giovanni explained what had happened to Lily, Thomas felt more relief than anger. He realized that it was Toby's quick thinking and Giovanni's skill that had saved his daughter from greater harm, and he was grateful.

"Doc, your service is valued more than you know. Without your skilled hands, this ship and its crew would suffer. My wife and I are in your debt."

If an Italian from Milan could blush, Giovanni showed a striking mix of pride and humility. The captain and the carpenter shook hands, and then Thomas turned to face Toby, who was shyly looking down at his own boots, hoping not to be noticed.

"Toby, you always give far more than is expected or required. When we dock at San Francisco, I am going to recommend you for a promotion. I think you'll make a fine seaman. Thank you for serving with distinction."

Toby looked up and flashed his boyish grin. "Thank you, Captain. It's an honor to watch over Lily."

The next day, when Sarah brought Lily to Giovanni's workroom, he greeted her with a small sack made of blue velvet.

"I have something you can play with inside your warm cabin. Now that we're south of the equator, it's winter in July! Open the bag and you'll find a good toy for cold weather."

Lily's eyes opened wide as she peered into the sack and emptied its contents onto Giovanni's oak table. Ten pointy pieces of pewter and one round wooden ball spilled out and scattered over the smooth surface.

"What are these?"

Giovanni laughed. "Haven't you ever played jacks before? It's an old game that has been played by children all over the world. These ten pieces were given to me when I was a boy in Italy. My grandfather was a silversmith, and he made these jacks out of solid pewter. I made the ball myself. I made it this morning just for you. Toby knows how to play, and he is going to teach you."

As Lily gathered up the ball and jacks and gingerly put them back in their blue sack, she didn't even notice that Giovanni had started to clean her wound. Resting in the palm of her hand, the little velvet bag felt like a pirate's treasure. She could hardly wait to share it with Toby.

Around the Horn, through frigid temperatures and horrible ice storms, Lily kept busy listening to stories, having tea with her doll, drawing with colored chalk, and playing jacks every afternoon with Toby. Whenever they played, Molly and her kittens were close by, and Moby and Midnight soon learned to chase the wooden ball and hold it in their paws.

Lily's leg healed beautifully with barely a scar, and the crew settled down once they passed around the Horn and reached Lima and the calmer waters of the Pacific. Everyone aboard, however, was more than ready to drop the ship's anchor when they finally arrived in San Francisco on the first of August. Thomas felt the whole crew deserved some rest and recreation, so as soon as they unloaded all of the coal, he announced that over the next fifteen days, all would be free to go ashore for five consecutive days on a rotating basis. The crew cheered when they heard the news, and then they drew straws to see who would go ashore first. The excitement was palpable.

Before leaving New York, Thomas had promised Sarah that he would take her to the best Chinese restaurant in Chinatown, and now it was time to deliver on that promise. On August 2, 1887, Thomas, Sarah, and Lily, dressed like Yankee royals, walked down the gangway and stepped into a hired carriage that took them directly to the Shanghai Dragon. For Sarah and Lily, it was like arriving at a foreign port. At the door, Lily gasped as she looked into the red eyes of an enormous gold dragon. Sarah's eyes widened as she spied a hundred dancing lanterns dangling over the tables. Later, the wait staff, dressed in black silk shirts over black silk pants, served them rice with chicken and vegetables, but much to Sarah's dismay there was no silverware. With unusual patience, Thomas showed Sarah and Lily how to use chopsticks. Sarah, of course, caught on quickly. Lily, on the other hand, tried hopelessly to grasp a little rice and raise it to her mouth. After a dozen attempts, she started to use her fingers. Sarah frowned in disapproval. She felt it wasn't proper for a captain's daughter to use her fingers to eat at a dining table, but Thomas tipped his chair back and laughed.

"It's better to eat with your fingers than not eat at all! Besides, we have to get back to the ship before sunrise!"

They all laughed at the thought of taking all night to eat their rice and chicken with chopsticks. It was an unforgettable night. Captain Goss and his family were out on the town, and they were enjoying every magical moment.

When the *Paul Revere* was fully loaded with a cargo of grain headed for Yokohama, and all hands on deck were prepared to haul anchor, Thomas noticed that his crew looked exhausted. Clearly, they had sacrificed rest for the sake of amusement while on shore. Even Toby looked tired, and he was about to begin his duties as a sailor. San Francisco was an enchanting city, but it was not without sin. A few weeks later, several sailors were stricken with high fevers. With all of the tonics, rubs, and mysterious treatments that he had learned in the Caribbean, along the River Plate and among the indigenous peoples of Chile and Peru, Giovanni tried to heal them, but nothing seemed to work. More than a dozen sailors lay listlessly in their bunks. The fever was spreading fast, and he alerted the captain.

At the risk of frightening Sarah, Thomas suggested that Lily keep her distance from the crew, including Toby. Even though Toby's duties aboard ship had changed, he still managed to visit Lily. When he came aft to her cabin, he usually had Moby or Midnight tucked under his coat. Lily was forever looking for the cats, and it was Toby who always knew where to find them. Sarah knew it would be impossible to keep Lily away from the sailors, especially Toby. But Lily became ill before her father had a chance to forbid her to mingle with the sailors on the quarterdeck. Giovanni tried every trick he knew to break her fever, but over the course of a month, her condition only worsened. With Thomas and Sarah's permission, Toby remained at Lily's bedside as if he was indeed her guardian angel.

Seven weeks after leaving San Francisco, Giovanni pressed his ear to Lily's chest and whispered in quiet resignation, "Her lungs are filling with water. She's drowning."

Sarah began to sob. Thomas tried to comfort her, but she was inconsolable. Desperate to save his little girl, Thomas pushed Giovanni aside, picked up Lily, his little feather, and carried her to the helm of the ship. Looking up at the vast blue sky, he cried, "Why not me? Take me instead!"

The sea and the sky did not reply.

CHAPTER 21

1887–1888

When word spread aboard ship that the captain had lost his little blue feather, tough, hard-nosed sailors wept, and the mighty *Paul Revere* fell silent. When five of their shipmates died, they were saddened, but when Lily died, they were broken.

Three days later, the *Paul Revere* arrived at Yokohama's busy port, and she dropped anchor like a ghost ship. As soon as the cargo was unloaded, Toby and Giovanni both asked to be transferred to another ship. In a private meeting, Toby told his captain that he felt Lily's presence aboard ship, and at night he thought he saw her running toward the forecastle to look for Moby and Midnight. Giovanni also met with the captain to explain his request for a transfer, but after starting and stopping several times, he suddenly broke down and cried. Feeling the same gut-wrenching sorrow, Thomas patted Giovanni's shoulder and handed him the blue velvet bag that he had given Lily just a few months earlier. The carpenter pressed the little bag of jacks to his chest, bowed his head and left the captain's cabin.

Thomas himself went ashore to arrange for Lily's last passage. He was familiar with the port of Yokohama, and he knew a reputable Japanese embalmer who would be willing and able to help. He also knew that Captain Daniel McGowan's schooner, the *Cassie F. Bronson*, was in port. The ship's familiar presence in the harbor consoled him. The Bath-built schooner was getting ready to set sail for New York in a day or two, and Thomas was counting on his good friend to carry Lily swiftly home.

He met with Daniel at a tavern, and they tossed back several shots of whiskey before discussing the passage from Yokohama to New York. Of course, Daniel agreed to help his friend. He also offered to arrange for the train ride from New York to Bath. With great tenderness, he promised that a member of his crew would stand guard over Lily's body until they reached New York's safe harbor and that the *Cassie F. Bronson* would be blessed with fair winds and following seas because Lily's spirit would be sailing with them. The hour was late, and Thomas was exhausted. He looked at Daniel's kind, strong face, and breathed slowly in and out before attempting to speak.

"I can barely remember our carefree college days at Bowdoin. How could we have known that one day we would be sitting together halfway around the world talking about my daughter's final passage? I'm finding it hard to breathe."

Daniel looked into his empty glass and said, "Lily is with God, and she is telling him to help you breathe. He holds you both in the palm of His hand, and He always will. Now, go back to the ship and rest. I will bring Lily home."

The next day Daniel came aboard the *Paul Revere* and went directly to the captain's quarters to pay his respects to Sarah. He knocked lightly on her cabin door and was surprised when she opened it. She looked remarkably thinner and paler then he remembered her, but her eyes were still intensely blue. He gave her a strong hug, and she allowed him to hold her for a full minute before she stepped back and handed him a letter addressed to her sister, Celia.

"Please give this to my sister when you reach Bath. I'm sorry I can't visit longer with you, but I'm not myself. I know you understand."

Without hesitating, Daniel bowed and backed away. "Of course, Sarah, I'll let you rest."

Thomas met Daniel on the quarterdeck, and together the two Yankee captains from Bath carried Lily's small coffin off of the *Paul Revere* and onto the *Cassie F. Bronson* for the long passage to New York and home. Neither Thomas nor Daniel knew what Sarah's letter said, but months later Celia would read it and stain it with her tears.

Dear Celia,

Tonight I write the saddest words. Our star has left the sky. I am sending you the remains of our sweet Lily. Please bury her on Beacon Hill next to Mama and Papa. Her soul is with God, and my heart goes with her.

Your loving sister,
Sarah

* * *

When the *Paul Revere* hauled anchor two weeks later, over half of the original New York crew had been replaced. DeGroote and Peck, the ship's owners, advised Thomas to hire a less expensive crew in Japan. Even though Thomas usually opposed such unfair practices, he had no choice. Faced with the deaths of five sailors and transfer requests from several others, Thomas hired a dozen sailors at Yokohama's busy port, and they were definitely cheaper. Unfortunately, they also lacked experience.

Despite the sun's rising every day, the voyage became dark and dreary. Sarah didn't speak. In the aftermath of Lily's death, she retreated into a gloomy silence and spent her days knitting without purpose. Her icy blue eyes, the same eyes that less than a decade before had captured Thomas's heart and turned him into a married man, now terrified him. To avoid those cold eyes, he paced the deck inspecting every nook and cranny and every sailor's knot. Of course, the crew found such scrutiny unnerving, and their performance dropped from mediocre to poor.

As the mood aboard ship darkened, so did the forecast. The *Paul Revere* reached Cape Hatteras on February 4, 1888, and the North Atlantic was angry. From the Carolinas to New York City, the tired wooden ship sailed through howling winds and a blinding blizzard. One sailor was washed overboard by a blasting wave, and three others were injured when they were knocked down by strong gales, but the most terrifying moment of the storm occurred when Thomas found Sarah unconscious on the floor next to their bed. He noticed the bloodstain as he lifted her, but he didn't have time to dwell on its meaning. Sarah needed a hospital, and that hospital was sixty nautical miles away. His ship would have to fly!

Even at the hands of an inexperienced crew, the Bath-built ship flew through the water. If it had not, Sarah Gannett Goss would not have survived. As soon as they docked, Sarah was taken to Bellevue Hospital. Thomas held her hand in the ambulance and never stopped talking.

"Sarah, I'm here. You're going to be all right. Stay with me. I need you. We're almost there. Bellevue is the best hospital in New York…"

When they arrived at the hospital, Sarah was whisked away, and Thomas was left to wait alone. After what seemed like an eternity, a doctor opened the door and called Thomas's name.

"Thomas Goss?"

"I'm Thomas Goss. How's my wife?"

"I'm Doctor Gibbons. Your wife is stable. We stopped the bleeding, and I'm confident she is going to recover. I'm sorry we couldn't save the baby, a boy."

"Baby?" said Thomas in a quiet voice that screamed he didn't know.

"Yes. Why do you look so surprised?"

"Our voyage was marked by tragedy. Five months ago we lost our daughter to pneumonia."

"I'm deeply sorry, Captain Goss. I estimate your wife was six months pregnant."

Thomas's back straightened. He pinched the bridge of his nose, commanding himself not to cry. He deliberately breathed in and out, and then he asked Doctor Gibbons, "When can I see Sarah?"

"You can see her right now. Follow me. I'll bring you back to the recovery room."

Thomas pulled back the white curtain to see Sarah sleeping soundly. For the first time in months, she looked like herself, soft and gentle. Thomas stepped close, took her hand, and kissed it gently. And then, in the privacy of his wife's hospital room, he allowed himself to cry.

CHAPTER 22

2015

I could smell the bacon from the top of the stairs, and that meant Ty was probably whipping up his signature breakfast. My hand slid over the hard, smooth wood of the bannister as I rushed downstairs to taste those buttermilk pancakes! It was spring break, and Ty and I would be together for nine wonderful days before he had to go back to Baltimore. I'd never recommend splitting time between two cities. It's not ideal. Truth be told, I was finding the separation hard to bear, but today was a happy day. And maybe tomorrow Ty would decide to retire, and we'd be together again full-time!

As soon as I stepped into the kitchen, Ty presented me with a steaming cup of coffee and a winning smile.

"It's a beautiful day to be in Maine!"

I stood on my toes and kissed him on the cheek. "It's sweeter with you here."

"If you keep talking like that, we'll have to skip breakfast and go back upstairs."

"Oh, honey, we can't do that. These pancakes look

too delicious to miss. Besides, we have nine whole days, and we should pace ourselves."

I set the table and poured two glasses of orange juice while Ty flipped the last few pancakes before we both sat down to enjoy an easy Saturday morning.

"Remember," Ty teased, "we only have nine days to eat all these pancakes, so let's pick up the pace."

"You're incorrigible! You know that, right?"

"No, but I have a feeling you're going to convince me."

I had to laugh. "Honey, these pancakes are the best! I've missed you."

As he reached for his morning newspaper, he replied with a wink, "And I've missed you. It's good to be home. It's so good that I've been thinking about our next chapter."

"Please tell me you're thinking about retiring."

Ty nodded. "I am. One of my colleagues is retiring, but he's going to teach part-time as an adjunct professor in Florida. That really appeals to me. Heck, I'm not ready to stop teaching, but I want to live in Maine and be with you every day of the year. Maybe I could teach a class at Bowdoin or Bates."

"Now you're cooking—no pun intended! Bowdoin's library is probably open today. Why don't you visit? Doris is coming over later to show us NPI's research on the history of our house, but you don't have to be here. Doris and I will enjoy some girl talk while you peruse the books at Bowdoin!"

"Why do I think you've been planning this all along? But okay. Now relax and savor this hot breakfast!"

As I took my last bite, my iPad beeped to announce a new message. It was from Anna. Her timing was perfect. I shared it with Ty right away.

Mom, it's another foggy day in Tacoma, but we're shooting inside the high school, so the weather doesn't matter. All is going well. Jeff Logan is bringing Wyatt Jones to life. As my

*Tacoma detective, he's smart, handsome, and sometimes gruff.
And I think I love him! Just kidding, but remind me to send the
casting agent some Maine lobsters! XO Anna*

When I finished reading, I looked up at Ty and smiled. "I can almost hear her shouting 'Hooray!' I think our daughter has found her happy voice again."

Ty leaned back in his chair and whispered, "Amen."

* * *

The doorbell rang and I heard "Jingle Bells." Whatever the season, whenever anyone rings our doorbell, it plays "Jingle Bells." Ty won't let me change it. I guess he's hoping it will keep us merry. So far, it's working. I opened the door with a smile.

"Good morning, Doris! By any chance is that envelope in your hand for me?"

"Yes! Of course it's for you. Nequasset Preservation, Inc., has officially completed your house history, and it's fascinating!"

"Come on in and tell me about it. Who built this house, and when did they build it? Wait! This calls for a cup of tea."

"And a scone!" added Doris.

"Ah, yes. The blueberry-lemon scones are waiting for us on the kitchen counter."

Doris paused to listen. "Are you playing Simon and Garfunkel on the radio?"

"I am, but it's on my iPad, not the radio."

"Same difference!" quipped Doris with a little shrug.

And much to my surprise, she started to sing along:

*Cecilia, you're breaking my heart
You're shaking my confidence daily
Oh, Cecilia, I'm down on my knees
I'm begging you please to come home
Come on home…*

As I listened, I wondered if there was anything

Doris Van der Waag didn't do well. And when the song ended, I applauded.

"I didn't know you could sing! You certainly know how to call someone home. I love that song, and I've noticed they've been playing it a lot lately."

Doris grinned. "I love it, too."

"Since we've been married, Ty and I have lived in five different cities, but this is the first one that has made us feel like we truly belong."

"I know that feeling," said Doris gleefully. "Living in Bath is like getting a hug from your grandmother every day, and who wouldn't feel nurtured by that kind of love?"

I nodded and said, "That's so true!" Then I reached for my scalloped green plates, the ones that were embossed with a mother bee.

Doris gasped. "Where did you get these dishes? I want them!"

"Anna gave them to me for Mother's Day last year. She knows I have a weakness for tableware. I think she found them at an antiques store. Anna has exquisite taste, and she buys the best gifts!"

"I adore my three boys," Doris sighed, "but a daughter adds a little extra honey to everyday life. You're lucky, Ellie. Now where should I take my cup of tea?"

"Let's go into the sunroom and pretend the sun is shining!"

We sat down on my favorite wicker chairs. They were painted a bright coral, so I called them my mermaid chairs. I loved their downy-soft cushions, and Doris loved their name.

"My goodness, Ellie, whenever I sit in one of these chairs, I imagine your garden blooming with black-eyed Susans, purple coneflowers, and pink hydrangeas. And I'm reminded how summer never fails us. It comes every year!"

I laughed. "Doris, I'm glad you're here! You are sunshine on a cloudy day! But before we discuss the history of the house, I have to tell you that I just received a text from Anna, and the filming is going well in Tacoma. Apparently, Tori Vega and Jeff Logan have great on-screen chemistry."

Doris raised her tea cup as if it were champagne. "Here's to Daisy Longtree, the medicine woman, and Wyatt Jones, the smart detective who relies on her."

I raised my cup in agreement. "And I think Daisy and Wyatt are going to make Anna Malone famous!"

Doris's face suddenly lit up. "You know, Ellie, it's possible this old house inspired Anna's screenplay."

"How could that be?"

"Remember when Anna thought she saw two female ghosts in her bedroom?"

"Yes, I remember. And she woke up thinking about the name Cecilia."

Doris opened her eyes wide and whispered, "Maybe that Simon and Garfunkel song that keeps playing on your iPad is sending us a message. I think Celia, which is a form of Cecilia, may be Anna's muse. There's a definite connection between the history of this house and Anna's new screenplay, *Daisy Longtree*. According to NPI's research, a woman named Celia Gannett owned this house at the turn of the twentieth century."

I sat speechless while I tried to process this improbable fact. "Well, if Celia's ghost visited Anna, who was the other female spirit?"

Doris smiled like a girl with a secret. "As fate and Bath would have it, Celia's sister, Sarah, lived with her because her husband was a sea captain, and he was at sea for years at a time."

"This is crazy! Next, you're going to tell me I should hire a shaman to rid my house of restless spirits."

Doris shook her head. "No, I'm simply suggesting that Anna wrote her best screenplay to date in Bath, and that the history of this house may have inspired it. I don't think it's a coincidence that Anna's story takes place in Tacoma, Washington, because sea captains from Bath used to sail there, and sometimes their families sailed with them. And I'm not sure it's random that Anna's hero is not just a teacher, but a Native American medicine woman as well."

I put my tea cup down, and calmly said, "Oh, I see. You think the ghosts of Bath helped Anna imagine a spiritually sensitive Daisy Longtree. Really?"

Doris laughed. "It's just a theory, Ellie. But a lot of people believe the houses of sea captains are haunted. Like Hemmingway's bullfighters, they lived life full up, but they also endured tremendous hardships, and their families suffered great losses."

"I can appreciate that. But getting back to NPI's report, was this house built by a sea captain?"

"No, it was built by a sea captain's son, Thomas Agry, in 1823. When we realized your house was built prior to the formation of Sagadahoc County, we followed the deed trail back to the Lincoln County Courthouse and discovered that your house was originally built a block from here on the corner of Pearl and Washington Streets. It was moved to its present location in 1856 by Captain Henry Goss and his wife, Charlotte."

I listened while Doris explained how NPI traced the deed to our house back to the boom years of Bath's shipbuilding history, and I learned that our house had been owned and cared for by not one, but many shipbuilders and shipmasters. It was a lot to take in at one sitting, and my head was spinning with names and dates, but I was beginning to believe that Ty and I had purchased a Maine maritime treasure.

I glanced at my watch and realized it was almost eleven o'clock, and I was supposed to be over at the library to discuss plans for the Memorial Garden with the city's historians.

"Doris, I have to run to a meeting, but I promise I'll pore over this report. NPI has done a fabulous job. I think you've discovered some buried treasure!"

"Wait! I have to show you the best gem. I found a

photograph online and printed a copy for you. It's a picture of Captain Henry Goss when he was about fifty years old."

I stared at the rugged, handsome face of a clearly confident man. He was looking straight into the camera lens with bright, soulful eyes, and he was sporting a stylish goatee without a mustache. His white hair was thick and wavy, and a bit unruly. He looked rather dashing in a Johnny Depp kind of way, and for some unknown reason I felt as if he were about to speak to me. And then Doris interrupted my daydream.

"What do you think of our Captain Goss?"

"I think he's fascinating, and I want to get to know him better, but now I really do have to go. We'll have to talk again about the captain."

I followed Doris out the front door, waved goodbye as she hopped into her old Volvo wagon, and hurried down the street toward the library. As I passed by the Inn at Bath on the corner of North and Washington, I felt my phone vibrate. When I pulled it out of my pocket, I saw that it was Frank calling.

"Hi, Frank. How's Boston?"

"Hot!" my son answered. "I mean, unbearably hot. Would you mind if I drove up with Tess tomorrow? We'd like to get out on the water and paddle!"

"Your canoe is always waiting for you. And you never have to ask your mother for an invitation. Come on up!"

"Thanks, Mom. By the way, I made something for your birthday. I think you'll like it."

"Are you building me a canoe to match yours? You know, I think you've missed your true calling. You could be a shipbuilder."

"Funny, Mom! But this time I didn't use my saw. I decided to use my iPad skills instead, and I researched our family history and mapped it all out on a chart."

Frank, my blond, beach-boy son, never failed to surprise me with his kindness.

"That's amazing. I can't wait to see it."

"Well, I can give you a quick fact that will pique your interest. Your mother, Stella Donavan, was born in Bowdoinham, Maine, but her father, Thomas Goss, was born in Bath! How's that for an uncanny coincidence?"

I came to a complete stop and asked, "Did you say Captain Henry Goss?"

"No, I said Thomas Goss, but his father was Henry Goss. How did you know about him?"

Stunned, I looked up at the elegant bandstand in the middle of City Park, and my thoughts turned back to the Agry, Goss, and Gannett families who had lived in my house, each for a significant period of time over a century before, and I whispered, "Holy Mary!"

CHAPTER 23

1888

It was snowing as the train pulled into Brunswick. Thomas looked out of the frosted windows and saw the sprawling campus of Bowdoin College sparkling in the chill of the winter day. The tall, snow-capped evergreen trees seemed to be standing guard around the Federal-style red-brick buildings, and he felt instantly at home. When he caught a glimpse of the chapel's steeple, his thoughts turned to that fateful day when he had decided to leave school and go to sea. Looking back, Thomas thought about how different his life would have been had he not gone to sea with Captain Sam Gannett. Would he have met and married Sarah? Would he have lost a daughter and son? If he had chosen a different path to his future, would his wife still be sharing his bed? He had always hated *if* questions, but today he found them unbearable.

As the train came to a full stop, he spotted his mother and father waiting on the platform. He was surprised to see his mother because she usually stayed home to prepare a big meal while his father met them at the station.

On this occasion, a time of deep sorrow, Charlotte must have felt that Sarah needed a mother's arms to welcome her. Thomas sighed. Charlotte Goss was the most intuitive person he knew.

Thomas stepped off the train first, then he turned and reached back to help Sarah, who looked unusually pale. Without waiting for any verbal acknowledgment, Charlotte gathered Sarah's thin torso in her arms and pressed her to her bosom as only a mother can do. Sarah buried her face in her mother-in-law's shoulder and seemed to crumble in her loving embrace. Charlotte held her for as long as she could without causing a scene.

Once in the carriage and on the way home, Charlotte said, "Your sister is preparing a delicious dinner for all of us back at the house. Even better, she is planning to stay with us for a while. In fact, Celia has expressed an interest in buying our house on Washington Street when Henry and I move to Staten Island. The company wants Henry selling their ships at New York Harbor all year long, and Celia had this brilliant idea that you and Thomas could share this lovely old house with her. If you consider all the time that Thomas spends at sea, I think it's a perfect plan."

For the first time since losing Lily, Sarah looked up with curious, wide-open eyes. "Really?" she whispered.

Charlotte laughed nervously. "Yes, really! Oh my dear, we have so much to talk about."

Sarah didn't say another word, but Thomas noticed a flicker of light in her blue eyes that he had not seen since Lily's heart stopped beating. Charlotte Goss was known for her tender spirit. Thomas suddenly realized that if anyone could restore his wife's will to live, it was his mother because she knew the sorrow of losing a child—she had lost two, also. Thomas leaned toward his mother and kissed her on the cheek. "I've missed the sound of your voice. Sarah and I have never needed your love more than now."

"Welcome home, Thomas. Keep looking up, and be patient. There's lots of blue sky in your future."

Less than an hour later, Thomas opened the door of the Goss's home and glimpsed Celia walking down the winding staircase. As she touched the smooth wood of the handrail, Thomas's mind filled with memories of his youth. He could almost hear his brothers, Jonathan and Francis, calling his name, daring him to slide down that splendid bannister. He also remembered Celia as the feisty young lady he had met on the deck of *El Capitan*. She was the one who had encouraged him to stand up to her cruel brother.

"Hello, Thomas!" called Celia as she quickened her step to meet him, and then she glimpsed her sister behind him. "Oh, Sarah, is it really you? You're home at last!"

As soon as Celia wrapped her arms around her, Sarah began to sob uncontrollably. For months she had willed herself not to cry because she was afraid that if she started, she would never be able to stop. From Calcutta to the North Atlantic, from Cape Hatteras to New York Harbor, Sarah had felt she was losing her mind. When she lost her baby at Bellevue Hospital, she wanted to die. Now, in the safety of her sister's warm embrace, she wailed in pain and rage.

Celia rocked her gently and whispered in her ear, "It's all right, Sarah, let it go, let it go. That's right, let it go."

The entrance hall was filling with afternoon light as Thomas observed the healing power of a sister's love. He swallowed hard and pinched the bridge of his nose, willing his own tears away. Charlotte and Henry stood side by side and watched the homecoming unfold with a reverence usually reserved for church. When Sarah's sobbing finally slowed, Charlotte reached out and touched her shoulder.

"My dear, your room is ready. We put up the wallpaper that you chose before you left. Remember? It has little yellow daffodils with light-green stems on a creamy white field. Why don't you go up and climb into that big bed, crawl under those soft quilts, and rest? You've had a long journey, and you must be exhausted."

Celia agreed. "I stoked the fire just as you arrived. It's warm and cozy up there. You're home, Sarah!"

Arm in arm, the Gannett sisters climbed the stairs with hungry hearts. Together they prayed that the Goss's sunny old house could fill them up with the hope they desperately needed.

A few minutes later, Celia came down and found Thomas in the living room. His left arm was leaning on the carved wooden mantel of the fireplace, and he was staring at the hot, shooting flames. Lost in thought, he didn't notice when Celia entered the room.

"Thomas," said Celia quietly, "I wish there was something I could say or do to comfort you."

"You already have. You opened your arms to Sarah, and she opened her heart to you. That's the first time I've seen Sarah cry, or show any feeling, since we docked at Calcutta."

"And how are you surviving, Thomas?"

"I'm not sure that I am surviving. Sarah refuses to let me touch her. We've not shared a bed since Lily died. I didn't even know about the baby. We must have conceived our son in San Francisco."

Without thinking, Celia approached Thomas and put her hand on his cheek.

"I'm sorry, Thomas. Our hearts are all aching, but time will help us heal."

Thomas lowered his gaze, looked into Celia's misty eyes, and whispered, "I know, I know. It will. It must."

Suddenly, Celia realized her hand was still cupping Thomas's cheek, and she quickly placed it over her own heart and stepped away from the fire.

"Do you have any plans?" she asked in an unusually high voice.

"No, I've thought about retiring from the sea, but I'm not sure. Captain Robert McGowan, my father's old friend, wrote to me when he heard of Lily's passing, and he invited Sarah and me to visit him and his second wife, Catherine, at their farm in Bowdoinham. Robert retired years ago and has no regrets. I'm too young to retire, but I believe Sarah needs me, and I doubt she will ever go to sea again."

Celia listened attentively, then she offered Thomas her opinion. "Perhaps you should go to Bowdoinham and stay with the McGowans for a while. I can keep Sarah distracted with a new quilting project, and we can practice our music. Maybe you should take some time to clear your head and plan your future."

"Ah, Celia, you are the wisest of the wise. I'll take your sage advice."

Even in sorrow, Thomas knew how to be charming. Celia shook her head and smiled. Looking into his warm brown eyes, she was convinced there was hope, and she was convinced that Thomas needed time away from Sarah and the whole family in order to work through his own grief.

* * *

When the lilacs started to bloom, Thomas heeded Celia's advice and borrowed his father's wagon to go to Bowdoinham for a visit with the McGowan family. Spring is unpredictable in Maine, but May 27, 1888, was a clear, sunny day, and Thomas was not in a hurry. For most of the trip along dirt roads framed by bending birches and tall evergreens, he let the horses trot at a slow and steady pace and enjoyed the ride. Feeling relaxed for the first time in months, he started to sing "Blow the Man Down."

When he was a boy, he had often listened to the riggers sing as they worked high up on the tall ships just a hundred yards from his bedroom window, and "Blow the Man Down" had been his favorite song. At the time, he didn't fully understand the lyrics, but now he could sing them with all the sanguine emotion of a drunken sailor. As he sang the words in a deep, salty voice, he was reminded of the cruelty of his first captain, Sam Gannett, and of all the beatings he had witnessed as a mate aboard *El Capitan*. "Blow the Man Down" was not alluding to men being knocked down by stormy seas; it was suggesting that sailors were often mistreated aboard ship.

On this sunny day in May, Thomas thought only the evergreens would hear his soulful music, but someone was riding behind him on a beautiful chestnut mare, and she heard every word and recognized the song because her father sang it, too. What Mary Rose McGowan did not know was that the song had a double meaning for Thomas. In fact, she didn't know Thomas at all. If she had, she would have known that today he was thinking about his daughter, Lily, as he sang the riggers' work song.

When he heard Mary Rose's creamy voice for the first time, he was dreaming of Lily playing with her Liverpool cat, Molly, and her two kittens.

"Are you lost?" asked Mary Rose as she slowed her horse to a trot.

Thomas looked left and saw a young girl with midnight-black hair and ivory skin riding beside him, and for a moment he was speechless. "No, I'm on my way to Captain Robert McGowan's farm in Bowdoinham. If I'm not mistaken, it should be a few miles up the road. And who are you?"

"I'm Mary Rose McGowan, the captain's daughter. And you must be Captain Thomas Goss, my brother's friend from Bowdoin College. I've heard a lot about you."

"Well, I hope Daniel was kind. I'm not as bad as those Bowdoin stories suggest."

"No one could be that bad! In your defense, he did say that you were too handsome for your own good. From where I'm sitting, he was probably right about that."

"Now I am truly embarrassed. Perhaps you should tie that fine horse of yours to the back of this wagon and ride with me. I'd like to explain my bad behavior in college and convince you that I am a better man today."

As Thomas reined in the horses and brought the wagon to a halt, Mary Rose dismounted. The morning light peeked through the bare branches of a towering tulip tree near the side of the road and lit up the girl's soft, round face. Thomas could see freckles across her small, upturned nose. Her eyes were mostly green, but some might call them hazel, and they were set wide apart under thick, long lashes and full, dark brows. Thomas remembered hearing the sailors in London talk about "black Irish beauties," and he knew instantly that she was such a beauty, a wild Irish rose.

"You're Captain Henry Goss's son, aren't you?" asked Mary Rose in an engaging way as she stepped up and lifted her slim, agile body into the wagon.

Unfortunately, Thomas didn't hear the question because he was busy admiring her graceful limbs, so Mary Rose rephrased it.

"Is it true that your father and my father are considered two of the best Yankee sea captains ever to command a Bath-built ship?"

Thomas tilted his head back and laughed as if he were twenty again. "Yes! That would be true!"

Mary Rose was quiet for a moment before coyly asking, "How old are you?"

Thomas was clearly surprised. "I must be twice as old as you. I'm thirty-three."

"Really? You look a little older than thirty-three."

Thomas feigned injury. "The sea will do that to a man."

Mary Rose glanced at Thomas and casually said, "I'm eighteen, but I feel older. Did you know that my father admires Captain Henry Goss more than any other sea captain he has ever met? And one day I asked him why he felt that way."

Now Thomas was looking at Mary Rose's full red lips and listening to every word they formed. "What did he say?"

"He said your father had suffered a heartbreaking loss, a sorrow that could have destroyed him, but didn't."

"What else did he say?"

Mary Rose sighed. "If you know my father at all, you know he is Irish to the core and often relies on old Irish sayings to explain the most important mysteries. So to explain your father's remarkable goodness, he told me that 'Sorrow can burn you to bitterness or spin you to gold,' and that's all he said."

Tears started falling, and Thomas didn't try to wipe them away. He gripped the reins with both hands.

Mary Rose was stunned by his reaction, but she kept her eyes on the road ahead and didn't say another word until they arrived at her parents' farm.

When they heard the wagon, Robert and Catherine McGowan both came out of the house to welcome Thomas, and they were surprised to see their daughter with him.

"So I see you've met our Mary Rose!" shouted Robert as he hugged Thomas and pounded his back as if he were a long lost son. "Holy Christmas, you look like Henry!"

That evening, Catherine made a fabulous Yankee dinner. Thomas's plate was heaped with pot roast, red cabbage, boiled potatoes, and popovers with lots of butter. For dessert, Catherine served apple crisp topped with whipped cream, and Robert kept filling Thomas's glass with the best whiskey in the house, which made the room glow like a candle in the night. After dinner, they sat around the big oak table and discussed the business they all loved, shipbuilding. Robert begged Thomas not to retire from the sea. If Sarah's Uncle Arthur was willing to give him command of one of his new four-masted barks, he should accept. Robert believed the rumors that were flying around Long Reach were true. Arthur Gannett and Company was planning to build four big sailing ships, they were going to sail like "daisies wearing oilskins," and they might well be the last of the beautiful American sailing ships made of wood. By nightfall, Robert's passion convinced Thomas to bide his time and wait for the *Susquehanna*.

Thomas stayed ten days at the farm, and when it

was time to leave, he didn't want to go. As he harnessed the horses next to the barn, Robert advised him to keep active at the shipyard, and to keep watch over the *Susquehanna*'s construction. Finally, when it was time to say goodbye, Thomas choked. Robert embraced him before he turned and walked back to the house. Catherine had prepared a lunch for his trip, and she gave it to him with a sweet peck on the cheek. The only one left was Mary Rose. Thomas felt a wave of sadness wash over him. Like all sailors who go to sea, he knew that goodbye in any language sounds cold. There were really no words to express the pain of parting.

Mary Rose understood his silence. She reached up and kissed him tenderly on the cheek and said, "I'll miss you. Come back."

CHAPTER 24

2015

Thanksgiving is my favorite holiday because your presence is the only present required. This Thanksgiving our family felt especially blessed because we were all together. Stella, our first grandchild, and Tess, our newest daughter-in-law, were joining us for Thanksgiving dinner for the first time. The table was set with pretty dishes, sterling silver, and crystal glasses, and the centerpiece, a hollowed-out pumpkin filled with delicate white chrysanthemums and sweet-smelling eucalyptus, focused our attention on the beauty and goodness of our life. All we had to do was cook, eat, and talk all day long.

Anna was home, too. She had attended the premiere of *Daisy Longtree* on Friday, took the red-eye to Boston on Saturday, and then took the train up to Brunswick. She was exhausted, but she was also the happiest I had seen her in years. The early reviews were coming in, and they were glowing. Coastline Studios was ready to offer her an advance on her next project. Her associate producer had said she could ask Warren Dunlap for the moon, and he would try to get it for her. *Daisy* was a big hit, and we all wanted to celebrate.

Because the end of November is customarily the time for families to gather together to count their blessings, I chose November to dedicate the Bath Memorial Garden at the old Calvary Cemetery. On the Saturday after Thanksgiving, the sun was shining, and we could clearly see the red paving stones engraved with the names of Bath's founding families. The sinuous path led to an Arts and Crafts–style house that was about to become the garden's educational center, but in the early 1900s had served as the caretaker's home. Above the charming oak door with beveled glass, a small wooden sign read: A Quiet Place to Recall Our History. In the middle of the garden was a fountain with stone benches around it, and that's where a group of friends and family were gathering to celebrate a new beginning. We weren't launching a new, state-of the-art destroyer, but we were certainly launching an organization that was committed to preserving Bath's maritime history, and I felt lucky to play a role in such a maiden voyage.

Suddenly, Anna was standing beside me.

"Looks like you've found your secret garden after all, Mom."

"Yes and no," I replied quietly.

"What do you mean?" asked Anna with one eyebrow raised in her inimitable way.

"It's not mine, and it's not a secret. It belongs to the City of Bath. But yes, I feel as though I have found the right place to breathe deeply and enjoy an impressive view of present and past. Did you see the stone wall on the south end of the garden? I'm going to plant heliopsis along it next spring."

"That's your signature, Mom. They'll be lovely."

"You're lovely, Anna. Growing up, you were always a ray of sunshine, and you still are."

For a fast second, Anna looked like she was going

to cry. She reached out and hugged me tight. "I love you, Mom," she whispered.

Those three little words were heaven-sent, and they were still ringing in my ears when Bill Marston's booming voice asked everyone to form a circle around the garden's new fountain and its crowning sculpture, *Yankee Captain at the Helm*, a magnificent work in granite and marble of a young sea captain in a pea coat, hair tied back with one free lock falling across his forehead, and eyes fixed on the horizon. In the late-autumn breeze, I heard Paul Revere's bell ringing from the top of the City Hall at exactly twelve noon, and that was Bill's cue to introduce me. While I listened to his kind words, I gazed at the captain chiseled in stone and thought of Captain Henry Goss and his son, Thomas. Suddenly, it was my turn to speak, and I called for remembrance.

In the tall shadow of the handsome stone captain, I told everyone that we should remember by name the great mariners who left home to sail around Cape Horn and around the world carrying cargo and dreams. In closing, I praised Bath's unique and glorious maritime history, and then I cut the ribbon that stretched across the fountain and over the captain's stone hands. The crowd applauded. Carole Frymark began to sing an old shanty song, "Shenandoah," and everyone listened until the final note, and then they filled the garden once more with applause.

Truth be told, I can't remember a single word I said before cutting the ribbon, but Anna captured the moment on video, and Ty assured me every word made sense.

Joe gave me a one-arm hug. "Mom, you put a lot of good into this morning. You certainly know how to spin a story and pull some heartstrings."

I hugged him back, kissed him on the cheek, and whispered, "Thank you!"

Frank came over to praise my words, too.

"You cast a silvery net around us all, Mom!"

"Oh, Frank, it's the blarney in me!"

We both laughed as we entered SOCA's Memorial Education Center to join the party that had already begun. As I walked into the newly renovated space, I noticed that the tall windows on the south and west walls were letting in the afternoon sun and the room was filled with light.

Anna and Doris were chatting away at the big table in the center of the room. I could tell it was a lively discussion because their hands never stopped moving. I suspect Doris was quizzing Anna about the premiere. My granddaughter, Stella, was sitting on her daddy's lap drinking a Shirley Temple from a sippy cup and giggling like a happy sailor! My two daughters-in-law, Natalie and Tess, were talking nonstop about their Christmas shopping, and Ty was at my side. It felt good to have the family together and to feel completely at home.

Ty grabbed my hand and whispered in my ear, "What do you say we take a long walk this afternoon over the bridge to Woolwich and back again?"

I threw back my head and laughed.

"I say yes, my dear!"

"We're not retiring, Ellie. We're just starting a new chapter."

For a moment, I forgot that Ty and I weren't the only two people in the room. I took a deep breath and kissed him long and soft on the mouth in front of everyone. And then I heard all of my adult children clear their throats simultaneously. Suddenly, the room went silent— then it erupted into hoots, whistles, and lots of clapping.

Surrounded by history, it wasn't long before the conversation turned to Frank's study of our family tree.

Joe opened the discussion. "Am I the last to know that my grandmother was the daughter of Thomas and Mary Rose Goss, and that Thomas Goss was the son of Captain Henry Goss, whose portrait is hanging on that wall over there?"

Anna seized the moment to poke her brother.

"Joe, you're the genius of the family. Of course

you're not the last to know. Dad found out this morning."

"That's true," added Ty, "but in my defense, this family has been busy planning a lot of huge events this past year, and I'm not fully retired, so it's hard to keep up with all the new discoveries our research team provides."

Natalie winked at Joe and said, "I second that emotion. Sometimes I think our whole family is one big think tank! But I would like to know more about my daughter's namesake, Stella Rose Donovan. She certainly sounds like a star."

And with that play on words, it was my turn. Clearly, the question they were afraid to ask was how Mary Rose McGowan stole Thomas Goss away from Sarah Gannett Goss. In their eyes, this love story was a telenovela, and I couldn't disagree. Sometimes truth is stranger than fiction. When Doris realized I was at a loss for words, she rushed in to save me.

"Yankee captains led fast and furious lives, and their voyages were riddled with danger, despair, and—too frequently—death. Worst of all, their nights were dark and lonely."

With Doris's help, I found my voice.

"I've been doing some research, and I've learned a lot about our maritime roots. From personal letters, newspaper clippings, and so many other records, I think I've pieced together a fairly accurate story. When we get back to our house I'll share it with you."

Ty leaned over and kissed me, and as I looked over his shoulder, I saw Anna stand up and walk toward the back of the room. A second later, Jake was standing beside her. Their bodies were tense, and they weren't smiling. I could see their lips move, but I couldn't hear what they were saying. I was sitting on the edge of my seat as if I was watching a stunning silent movie. Over the past year, I had seen Jake around town with more than a few attractive women, but his face had never looked as handsome or as intense as it did right now. As Anna and Jake kept talking, their bodies gradually relaxed, and shortly after that, they smiled at each other. I could see the flash from across the room. As Anna's mother, I could only hope.

* * *

Jake looked at Anna with his piercing blue eyes, and she felt the room spin. He leaned forward, and she held her breath as he whispered, "Everyone is talking about your movie."

Anna tilted her head so she could see Jake's face. Giggling, she asked, "Really? Everyone?"

"Yes," said Jake with a nod.

"Come on, Jake, you know my mom tends to exaggerate."

"That may or may not be true, but I get most of my intel from Doris, and she just told me that Hollywood is buzzing about *Daisy Longtree*. Apparently the early reviews are over the top, and the premiere was a huge success. Congratulations!"

"Thank you. I've enjoyed the work, and I feel as if I've found my voice again."

"I don't think you ever lost it," said Jake, putting his arms around her waist. "From the moment I met you, your voice has reminded me of a sweet-flowing brook."

Anna looked up at him in amazement. "There you go again. You're crafting your words like a poet." Then she dropped her eyes and said softly, "I've missed you."

Jake put a gentle hand under her chin and tilted her face upward so he could kiss her. After a long, slow kiss, he whispered, "I've been waiting for over a year to taste you again."

Anna giggled. "Patience is your best virtue."

"No, it's not my best," Jake said with a half smile. "If you come back, I could dazzle you with my many attributes."

Standing on her toes, Anna planted a kiss on his mouth. Then, clear as a bell, she said, "Rest easy, Jake. I'm coming back as soon as I can."

Jake pulled her close. "I love the sound of your voice!"

* * *

Over the next few days, my family and I spent countless hours sitting in our sunroom discussing the lives of the men and women who had once dwelled in our house. I began with Thomas Goss's affair with Mary Rose McGowan, which resulted in the birth of Stella Rose McGowan in 1908. After her mother and father legally married in 1920, she became Stella Rose Goss. The records of Arthur Gannett and Company showed that Captain Thomas Goss took command of the *Susquehanna* in 1891 and remained her captain for eight years. While Thomas was at sea, his wife, Sarah, and her sister, Celia, lived in the home that had once belonged to Captain Henry Goss and now belonged to us.

According to the Sagadahoc County Book of Deeds, Celia Gannett bought Captain Henry Goss's house on Washington Street after his death in 1890, and she owned the house until she died. If Sarah's tombstone in Section Two of the Beacon Hill Cemetery is accurate, she died on March 2, 1920, six years before her older sister. At least one local historian believes that Sarah died of a broken heart. Apparently, a neighbor heard Sarah say that she hated Mary Rose McGowan, and he recorded that quote in his diary. Celia, on the other hand, had a more forgiving spirit. After Sarah's death, she invited Mary Rose and Stella to come to Bath and live in the big, empty Goss house on Washington Street. And then, without hesitation, Celia gave Thomas her blessing when he told her of his intention to marry Mary Rose. They married on October 14, 1920. Mary Rose was forty-eight years old when she legally became a Goss; Thomas was sixty-five. Sadly, Thomas died in 1925, and Celia died one year later.

Doris found a newspaper article in the library's history room that included part of the eulogy Stella Rose gave in honor of her beloved Celia on November

2, 1926, at the Winter Street Church.

"Celia Gannett was a woman ahead of her time. She was smart and independent and had an amazing capacity to love unconditionally. When I was twelve years old, my Aunt Celia, as I lovingly called her, gave me a sextant and encouraged me to master the art of celestial navigation. She wanted me to travel around the globe, find my true north, and return home safely. Because of her love, I have the courage to do that, and I will."

* * *

Shortly before Celia Gannett died, she added a caveat to her Last Will and Testament that professed her love for Thomas Goss. She gave Mary Rose Goss and her daughter, Stella Rose, the right to live in her beautiful home on Washington Street until Mary Rose's death. Because of Celia's devotion to family, another generation of mariners would call Bath home.

In 1942, Stella Rose Goss joined the United States Navy as a nurse, and she served on hospital ships and naval bases in the Pacific theater during World War II. Even though she never returned to Bath to live, she always carried a photo of the house on Washington Street in her wallet, and she never forgot the kindness of her Aunt Celia.

My family listened to the story of our house with eyes and ears wide open, but there were too many facts to digest in one sitting, so I told them I would continue the tale at Christmas. My adult children seemed to be okay with that, but before they had to return to their work in other cities, Frank had one more question.

"I've been reading up on Bath history—"

Closing one eye, Joe interrupted him as older brothers like to do. "Why am I not surprised?"

Everyone laughed, and then Frank continued in his mild-mannered way.

"Is Captain Henry Goss one of the Bath shipbuilders who helped the Catholics when an angry mob burned down the Old South Church in 1854?"

"Yes," I answered. "He, along with Oliver Moses, came to the aid of the Catholics and helped them find a new place to celebrate mass."

Anna piped up. "I'm convinced that if tombstones and old houses could talk, they would tell us that people are mostly the same. And since Warren Dunlap is so enamored with my work right now, I asked if he would support a documentary film about the sea captains of Bath and their legacy."

"How did he react?" I asked cautiously.

"He told me to start as soon as possible! And I may have started yesterday. I was rummaging through Grandma's old trunk when I found a poem that Grandpa wrote during the war. It's dated November 25, 1943."

I slipped on my reading glasses as Anna handed me a tissue-thin sheet of paper, and I slowly started to read my father's words out loud.

> *Stella, starlight,*
> *You bring me home.*
> *On a dark night,*
> *I'm not alone.*
>
> *Stella, sweet belle,*
> *You call my name.*
> *The waves can tell*
> *We love the same.*
>
> *Stella, bright star,*
> *You shine above the salty deck,*
> *And from afar,*
> *I feel your kiss upon my neck.*
>
> *Sailing on a blue sea,*
> *I'm Captain of the* Solitaire,
> *And I am true to thee.*

I looked up from the faded words on the single sheet of paper that had been folded and sent so long ago. The tears that had been welling up began to spill, but I quickly brushed them away so I could focus on the family gathered around me.

"Anna, this is a gift. I feel as if you've found a missing link in our family history. Thank you!"

Anna smiled and reached over and grabbed my hand. "I'm glad I did something right for a change."

"Oh, honey, you do a lot of things right, especially this. You always manage to find the best gifts!"

My words seemed to puzzle Anna, so I tried to explain.

"You all know that I was born out of wedlock, but I don't think you realize how that affected me. Growing up in the 1950s, I worried that my parents might have married because of me. In those days, having a love child was scandalous, but I think my parents' indiscretion was forgiven because I was conceived during the war, an extraordinary time."

I looked down at my hands clutching the thin sheet of paper covered with my father's carefully written words. Ty, sitting beside me, gave me a one-arm hug. I took a deep breath.

"For me, this slip of paper validates my parents' love story and frees me from guilt. This poem is a joyful gift."

CHAPTER 25

1890–1892

Men who go to sea and the women who wait for them are often deeply religious, but they also tend to hold onto some old superstitions. Across time, mariners and their families have recognized the divine and magical power of the number three. Some believe in the Trinity, but even more believe that good luck and bad luck come in threes. In Bath, the City of Ships, 1890 was no exception to the rule of three.

Freddy Minott, the fastest delivery boy for Western Union, dropped his bicycle in front of the granite steps of the Goss home on Washington Street. When he firmly pressed the doorbell three times, the red-headed messenger was sweating and breathing hard because he had pedaled up and down the hills of Front Street, turned west on Pearl Street, and almost knocked Mrs. Larrabee down when he came around the corner to deliver an urgent telegram to Mrs. Sarah Goss and Miss Celia Gannett. Within half a minute, Miss Gannett, tall and slender with her thick, dark hair piled on top of her head, opened the mahogany door, and Freddy recognized her immediately. She was the nice sister, the one who smiled and waved whenever she was out gardening and you passed by her white picket fence. The other sister rarely smiled and never said hello, but Freddy thought she was pretty like the goddess he'd read about in his high school Latin class.

"Hello, Freddy. What important message do you have for us today?"

"Good morning, Miss Gannett, I'm sorry to disturb you, but I have a telegram from Captain Goss addressed to you and Mrs. Goss, and it's marked 'urgent.'"

"Oh dear, that sounds like bad news. My sister is resting upstairs, but I'll share it with her right away. Thank you for delivering it so quickly, Freddy."

"You're welcome, Miss Gannett. I hope the news isn't too bad."

Celia closed the door and flew up the stairs. Her soft petticoats brushed the top of each pumpkin-pine step. Her hand glided over the bannister as gently as if she were playing a harp, and under her breath she prayed that the telegram was simply letting them know that Thomas's new command, the *Challenger*, would get under way a few days late.

Along with a crew of quirky, talented riggers, Thomas had recently sailed Arthur Gannett and Company's *Challenger* down to New York Harbor after it was re-rigged. The ship had been completely dismasted by strong gales at sea, and Uncle Arthur had asked Thomas to oversee its re-rigging and consider taking command. Even though Thomas had been promised the *Susquehanna*, a stunning four-masted bark still under construction at the shipyard, he agreed to captain the *Challenger* for one voyage. He had felt alone and sad in Bath, as Sarah had barely spoken to him and had never touched him since Lily's death. Thomas had hoped that a year at sea would ease his pain.

Celia knocked softly at Sarah's bedroom door, waited a second, and then pushed it open to find Sarah dozing in her favorite rocker next to the corner window. The sun cascading through the blown-glass panes illuminated her sister's face, and in that moment, Celia could see Lily. Suddenly she realized why Thomas couldn't bear to stay home. Whenever he looked at his wife, he could see his daughter's rosebud mouth, high cheekbones, and silky blond hair. With Lily gone, the resemblance was unnerving.

"Sarah, wake up! I just received an urgent telegram from Thomas. I thought we should open it together, since it's addressed to both of us."

Sarah opened her eyes and tried to focus on her surroundings. In a groggy voice, she asked, "What's wrong?"

Celia ripped open the telegram. "I'm not sure, but this message from Thomas will tell us, and I suspect it's not good news."

My dears, with great sorrow I must inform you that my father died early this morning. By the grace of God, I was able to spend two days with him before his sudden passing. I doubt there will ever be a shipbuilder or shipmaster as good as Captain Henry Goss. I will accompany my father home. Please meet us at the Bath train station on Tuesday at two o'clock. Fair winds and following seas. Thomas.

* * *

Sarah gasped as she listened to her sister slowly and deliberately read aloud the painful news of her father-in-law's death. Now fully awake, her eyes welled up with tears and she pulled a lace handkerchief from the sleeve of her dark-green dress. Celia needed one, too, so Sara stood up and offered her one from the top drawer of her dresser. Celia thanked her with a hug, and that tender embrace seemed to give them both comfort and courage.

Sarah spoke first. "What can we do for Thomas and his mother? Charlotte has always been so kind to us. Now it's our turn to help her."

"I agree," said Celia, "and I have an idea. We should organize a city-wide reception to welcome Henry home and honor his Herculean efforts to put Bath on every maritime map. If you trace Henry's contribution to Bath shipbuilding all the way back to his first partnership with Ethan Sawyer, you will count more than two hundred ships to his credit. We all owe Henry so much. He's the kindest man I know. I'm sure his friends and neighbors will line the streets of Bath to show their love when he comes home at last."

For the first time in months, Sarah spoke with purpose. "All right, let's walk over to Uncle Arthur's office. He can help us spread the word. It's only three o'clock. He should still be there. And we have to send a message to Charlotte's sisters, Emma and Amy. They'll want to make plans, too. I'm sure Henry will be buried next to his sons in the Riggs family cemetery. We should also contact the Eastern Steamboat Company and request that their steamer, the *Samoset*, be available to transport Henry's body and the funeral party across the river to Georgetown. This is going to take a lot of coordination."

Celia looked at Sarah as if seeing her for the first time after a long separation.

"You lead the way, Sarah. I'll be right behind you!"

Celia followed Sarah down the stairs and out the front door. Uncle Arthur's office was just around the corner at the bottom of Cedar Street. In less than five minutes, they were walking through the door of the small Italianate building that sat in the middle of Long Reach's busiest shipyard. To Celia, it was a noisy, dusty place, but it was also surprising and vibrant. There was usually an emergency, a fight, or a celebration happening at Arthur Gannett and Company's office on Front Street. Whenever a new ship was ready to be launched, there was a christening, and some important person—preferably a lady—smashed a bottle of champagne across the hull of the ship before it slipped over the ways. One of Celia's fondest memories was the day she herself had christened the *Iroquois*. Today, there would be no such celebration.

Upon entering the office, Sarah immediately looked right to find her uncle, as usual, sitting behind his massive desk, which was buried under a mountain of blueprints.

Together, Sarah and Celia walked quietly over to their uncle's seat of power, his notorious swivel chair, and Sarah cleared her throat. "Uncle, we have sad news, and we need your help."

Visibly shaken by the news of Henry's death, Arthur assured his nieces he would take care of all the necessary arrangements. The shipbuilders, investors, and local merchants would all turn out to honor Henry on the day he returned home.

"I'm meeting with Galen Moses in an hour. I'll ask him to call an emergency session of the City Council, and we will make sure Bath is ready to honor Captain Goss by next Tuesday. I suggest that you both take a quick trip over to Riggsville tomorrow and help make the arrangements for Henry's burial. Catch the morning steamer, and talk with the captain about transporting the funeral party. Be sure to mention my name, and tell him I will cover the cost."

"Thank you, Uncle Arthur," said Celia and Sarah in unison.

Before turning to leave, Celia added, "We'll be on the *Samoset* at ten o'clock tomorrow morning. We'll express our sympathy to Charlotte's family, and we'll offer our assistance. I'm sure Charlotte's sisters are as devastated as we are."

* * *

Five days later, on a beautiful May afternoon, the Portland train pulled into Bath with an elegant mahogany casket carrying the body of Captain Henry Goss. His wife, Charlotte, and his son, Thomas, had accompanied the body from New York's Grand Central Station to Boston, and then on to Portland and Brunswick, and finally to Bath. When the train screeched to a stop at the station, a band of local fiddlers began to play. All of the master shipbuilders and all of the shipmasters who were not at sea were assembled at the platform along with most of the city's hardworking citizens. Arthur Gannett, Galen Moses, General Thomas Hyde, and Captain Samuel Percy boarded the train immediately to help Thomas carry his father's coffin from the freight car to the horse-drawn carriage that would take Bath's hero to the dock in a procession befitting a maritime king. At the dock, they would meet his last crew, the crew of the steamboat *Samoset*, and they would carry him down the Kennebec to Robinhood Cove, his final passage.

As Thomas passed the fiddlers, he heard a high sweet voice singing "Simple Gifts," his father's favorite hymn.

> *'Tis the gift to be simple,*
> *'tis the gift to be free.*
> *'Tis the gift to come down where we ought to be.*
> *And when we find ourselves in the place just right,*
> *'twill be in the valley of love and delight.*

When Thomas looked up, he locked eyes with Mary Rose McGowan, and his heart skipped a beat. In turn, Mary Rose's pale cheeks blushed cherry-blossom red, which Thomas noticed before he looked straight ahead at the hundreds of people along the route from Depot Square to the Eastern Steamboat Company's wharf, which was just south of Summer Street, where the new library was being built. With the help of his fellow pallbearers, Thomas lifted his father's casket, covered with red poppies, onto the black funeral cart. Once the casket was secure, the driver gently urged his team of horses to move forward.

As soon as the procession started, Charlotte Goss joined her son, and hand in hand they followed the cart up Front Street. Sarah and Celia linked arms and walked behind them, followed by Charlotte's two sisters, and they were followed by representatives of every industry in the city. At the emergency meeting of the City Council, Galen Moses had shared the tragic news of Captain Goss's death, and the outpouring of grief was unprecedented.

That day, under a clear blue sky, Thomas could see that all the flags in the city were at half mast, and work had been suspended at all the shipyards. As he clutched his mother's hand and held it close to his heart, he could hear the fife and drum corps of Bath High School playing "Yankee Doodle." Along the gravel street of his hometown, he saw Mr. Isaac Small, the old master carpenter at Goss and Sawyer, and Elisha Mallett, the master builder at Arthur Gannett and Company. All of the grieving friends and neighbors that were following his father's casket up Front Street reminded him of how much his father had been loved and admired. Without a doubt, his father had lived a good life.

Upon arriving at the dock, Thomas spotted Captain Robert McGowan and his son, Daniel, among the faces in the crowd, and for the first time, he used the sleeve of his shirt to wipe his tears away. In that moment, he remembered how Captain McGowan had brought his father home so he could be with his dying children, and he also remembered his year at Bowdoin College when he'd rowed on the crew team with Daniel and forged an enduring friendship.

"Mother, Captain McGowan and Daniel are over there. We must invite them to join us on the *Samoset*. I know Father would want them to accompany us to Georgetown."

Charlotte nodded. "Please do. We need all the hugs we can get, and the McGowan family knows how to hug."

When Thomas left the procession, Sarah's eyes followed him, and at the same moment he reached Robert and Daniel McGowan, Mary Rose reached them, too.

"Thomas," she said, "I am sorry for your loss. Your father was a giant in this city, and his talent and kindness will be missed."

Daniel chimed in, "My sister is right. Your father was one of the finest shipbuilders Bath has ever known. I fear that as he goes, so goes our fleet of majestic sailing ships."

Robert stood at attention looking straight ahead at the casket. One solitary tear slid down his cheek as he cleared his throat and attempted to speak.

"Thomas, there are no words to express my sorrow. Your father was a true friend, and a life at sea doesn't allow for many friends." He turned and hugged Thomas hard.

Overcome with emotion, Thomas whispered back, "I know that feeling, but today you and I are among friends. Help me bring my father home, Captain. The Goss family would like the McGowan family to join us aboard the *Samoset* for my father's final passage."

Celia and Sarah looked on as Captain McGowan, accompanied by his two children, boarded the steamer. Celia welcomed them with a wave, but Sarah turned away and looked out over the tidal waves of the Kennebec with sad eyes.

* * *

Eighteen months later, Thomas was standing on the deck of his new command, the *Susquehanna*, when he saw the signal flags go up on the *Shenandoah*, another four-masted bark in the Gannett fleet. It was unusual for a captain to ask permission to board a vessel at sea for the sole purpose of delivering a message, but that was exactly what Captain James Murphy was asking. Thomas gave his fellow Yankee sea captain his permission and braced himself for bad news. Jim Murphy was not smiling when he boarded the *Susquehanna* fifty miles from the port city of Le Havre, France. Thomas shook his hand and promptly invited him to his cabin, where he filled two short glasses with whiskey.

"Let me have it," he said quietly.

Jim handed him the letter. "It's from Captain Daniel McGowan."

Thomas unfolded the sheet of paper and silently read the neat cursive writing. When he looked up, his eyes were wet.

"Captain Robert McGowan died. Daniel wanted me to know. Our fathers were best friends."

"And if I'm not mistaken, you and Daniel are good friends, too."

"Yes, and I wish I weren't half a world away. I should be in Bath right now."

"You will be there as soon as the sea and wind allows, Thomas."

"I'll drink to that!" He tossed back a full glass. It was going to be a long voyage, and he hoped the whiskey would dull the pain.

* * *

When all the pink and purple rhododendrons were blooming on Washington Street, Thomas opened the front door of his boyhood home. He smiled as soon as he saw the bannister that he liked to picture in his mind when he was away. And then he let his gaze fall to the half table against the short wall under the stairs, and his eyes fixed on the envelope waiting on a silver tray. At that moment, Celia appeared at the top of the stairs.

"That letter arrived yesterday. It's addressed to Captain and Mrs. Thomas Goss and Miss Celia Gannett, but I thought you should be the one to open it. It's from Mary Rose McGowan."

"Good morning, Celia! It's great to see your smile on this beautiful summer day. Where's Sarah?"

"She's still sleeping. I'm glad you're home, Thomas."

"Thank you. It feels good to be home at long last. I should go up and wake Sarah with a kiss."

"No, let her rest. She hasn't been well lately. After your father died, she tried to be strong, to be herself again.

But when you went back to sea, she stopped trying. Yesterday, when that letter arrived, she told me her life had no purpose without Lily, and she went up to bed. She said she would rather be sleeping."

Thomas picked up the letter. "Why would this letter affect her so much?"

"I don't know."

"Well, let me read it. Maybe it will shed some light."

Dear Thomas, Sarah, and Celia,

You probably know by now that my father passed away. He died in his sleep, and I suppose that is a blessing. He is with my mother now, and he is finally at peace. Daniel left for New York shortly after the funeral. He took command of the Rappahannock *and set sail for Portland, Oregon, a few weeks ago. Our big old farmhouse feels empty, and to honor my father, I need to change that. Please come for a visit. Bowdoinham is pretty in the summer. You can spend some carefree days picking blueberries and catching fireflies. My father told me once that the Goss family and the McGowan family would always be entwined. I never asked why, but my father was usually right.*

Hoping to see you soon,
Mary Rose

When Thomas finished reading Mary Rose's note out loud, he turned to Celia and said, "We should go. It would be good for all of us to wake up to chirping birds and crowing roosters instead of hammers and saws. Your uncle's shipyard is only a hundred yards away, and it makes a lot of noise."

Celia put her hand on Thomas's shoulder and looked directly into his warm eyes.

"Mary Rose may be inviting all of us, but it's you she wants to see. Sarah and I will decline her invitation, but you can choose to go."

"Well, I'm not going anywhere until I talk to Sarah."

* * *

Determined to speak candidly with Sarah, Thomas climbed up the center staircase and entered their bedroom without knocking.

"Sarah, it's me. I'm home."

Sarah sat up in the bed, and Thomas sat down beside her.

"Hello," said Sarah in a mouse-like whisper.

"Darling, I've missed you. Come downstairs, and we'll make a big breakfast. I think a stack of blueberry pancakes dripping in maple syrup will help us start the day right. How does that sound?"

"Did you read that letter?"

"Yes, I did. Mary Rose invited us to her farm in Bowdoinham for a vacation. It might be nice to get out of the city for a while."

"I can't leave. I would miss Lily more in Bowdoinham. I like to wake up to the noise of the shipyard, and I love to hear the riggers sing their shanty songs because their music reminds me of Lily's happy days aboard the *Paul Revere*."

Sarah began to cry and then sob uncontrollably. Thomas held her in his arms and rocked her like a baby.

"Hush, my darling. Lily would want us to be happy."

Still sobbing, Sarah struggled to put her words together. "Be happy for both of us. My heart hurts too much. You can't fix it, and I can't love you the way you need to be loved. Go to Bowdoinham, Thomas. Find some peace."

Thomas buried his face in his wife's soft, golden tresses and cried because he knew she was right.

"Whenever you need me, I'll be here."

"I know that Thomas. I do."

CHAPTER 26

1908

Back from another long voyage, Thomas tied his horse to a fence post near the McGowans' porch and walked up the creaky steps. He knocked on the screen door, but no one answered. As he waited, he looked at the porch swing and smiled. He had been gone for over a year, but he was no stranger to this place. After losing his precious daughter and his beloved father, he had started visiting the McGowan family on a regular basis. Now, standing at their front door, he remembered how Sarah had encouraged him to go that first time. She must have known that the McGowans would help him heal. And she was right. Sixteen years later, he was finally hopeful again, and he was anxious to see Mary Rose.

Thomas peered through the door and hollered, "Is anybody home? It's Thomas."

The silence was a bit unnerving. It seemed as if the old farmhouse, with its broken shutters and chipped paint, was still mourning its kind and caring owner, Captain Robert McGowan.

After knocking a few more times, Thomas decided to look in the barn. He thought Mary Rose might be busy cleaning the stalls, but the barn was deserted, so he walked to the back of the house, and that's where his eyes fixed on the prettiest sight he had seen in months. Mary Rose was standing next to the clothesline, and she looked like an angel as the blowing sheets engulfed her like clouds of white cotton. Thomas stood motionless and drank in her beauty like a sweet wine.

As Mary Rose bent down to touch the basket at her feet, she spied Thomas from the corner of her eye.

"Thomas! If that's you, you're an answer to my prayers! Come here and let me touch your face."

Thomas rushed over and wrapped an arm around Mary Rose's waist. As he took off his hat, he planted a firm kiss on her opened mouth. Pulling back, he said "It's me!"

"You shaved."

"Yes, I shaved for you." And he kissed her again.

Breathless, Mary Rose tried to speak, but her words were interrupted by a soft cooing sound that rose from the basket near her feet.

"Is there something other than laundry in that basket?" Thomas asked in a dazed voice.

Mary Rose responded by reaching into the basket and gently lifting up a smiling baby girl. "Thomas, this is your daughter. She has been waiting to meet you for almost five months, and I've been waiting even longer than that to tell you about this blessing."

Looking into his daughter's luminous eyes for the first time, Thomas was speechless. When he finally found his voice, he whispered, "Does she have a name?"

"Her name is Stella Rose."

"That's a beautiful name, and it suits her well. She's shining like a star already."

Thomas bent down and kissed his daughter's cheek ever so gently.

Mary Rose laughed. "This little one may be shining like a star, but she is definitely not smelling like a rose right now. Let's go inside. I'll change and feed Stella, and then I'll pour you a glass of sweet tea, and we can talk over a plate of my famous shortbread and sugar cookies. How does that sound, Captain?"

"If you let me carry Stella, it sounds like Christmas in July."

"Well, 'tis the season to be joyful! Hold out your hands, and I will gladly present you with our daughter."

Thomas cradled the baby in his arms and said, "I never dreamed that God would give us a child. What a miracle!"

Later, while Stella slept peacefully in her crib, Mary Rose and Thomas slipped out the front door and sat on the porch swing, which was directly below their daughter's window. If she cried, they would hear her from that sweet spot. Thomas had committed to a long voyage around Cape Horn before Mary Rose had had a chance to tell him she was pregnant. Now that he was back, she wanted to talk in earnest about all the changes that had occurred in his absence, but it was Thomas who started the conversation.

In a serious tone, he said, "Forgive me, my dear, but I have to ask you a question. Is my name on the birth certificate?"

"No, we aren't married, and our relationship has not been made public, but I have brought Stella Rose to the Winter Street Church, and she has attracted attention. There have been moments when I have felt as if everyone was staring at her. That is, everyone except Celia. She has been the kindest. Honestly, I think Celia knew I was pregnant before anyone else, including myself."

Thomas was nervous. He looked down at his hands, cleared his throat, and spoke haltingly. "I'm not surprised. She is incredibly observant and generous to a fault."

"That's so true. I would have been lost without her. When I called for the doctor, Celia came with him. She was present at Stella's birth, and she stayed with us for over a week to make sure we settled into a good routine."

Thomas listened quietly, then looked away to compose his thoughts. After a long pause, he reached for Mary Rose's hand. "If everyone could be as accepting as Celia, our world would be a more loving place, but I fear that will never be the case."

"What's wrong, Thomas?"

"I love you, Mary Rose, but I cannot marry you because I cannot add one more ounce of pain to Sarah's unending sorrow. She rarely speaks to me, and I know she still blames me for Lily's death and the loss of our infant son. If I hadn't taken them on that grueling voyage, they might be alive today."

Thomas stopped to clear his throat again, and Mary Rose leaned over to wipe a tear from the side of his face before he continued.

"In time, I hope to give Stella Rose the Goss name, but for now, I can only promise to love her all of my days. Next week, I will inform Arthur Gannett and Company that I will be retiring from the sea. Celia can watch over Sarah. My place is here."

Mary Rose rested her head on Thomas's shoulder. "Oh, my darling, don't worry. Our love will make it all right."

EPILOGUE

A part of me has always wanted to believe that movie magic could come true. And that's why I've seen *Night at the Museum* six times. I never tire of watching Robin Williams bring Teddy Roosevelt back to life. In Bath, I love to imagine Captain Henry Goss striding through the Maine Maritime Museum with plans for a new square-rig tucked under his arm. I know that's impossible, but tonight I went to see Anna's documentary, *The Mariners of Long Reach,* for the first time, and I believe that *was* a dream come true.

Upon arriving at the museum, I could feel the excitement. Doris was standing by the door with Seth Gray, the museum's director, and she quickly took Ty and me to our reserved seats in the front row. We glanced at each other as if to say, "Thank God Anna pays attention to details!" As we sat down, I noticed a poster on the east wall. It showed Anna, dressed in a white shirt and fitted black pants, aiming a camera at a new Zumwalt-class destroyer about to be launched. Ty noticed it, too. He pulled a clean handkerchief out of his pocket and handed it to me.

"Thank you," I whispered. "I think I'm going to need this."

"Don't worry," he said. "I brought two—one for you and one for me."

Without any introduction, the lights dimmed, and I waited to hear Anna's voice.

I looked up at the screen to see the City of Bath under a bright blue sky. The cameraman must have been in a boat, because that amazing view could only be captured from the water. I held my breath as the camera panned south to the Sagadahoc and Carlton Bridges, and then to the towering cranes of BIW. The camera continued to sweep southward to the Maine Maritime Museum and its full-size sculpture of the six-masted schooner *Wyoming*. Turning north, the camera lens captured the historic Customs House, the bell tower of City Hall, Waterfront Park, the shining spire of the Winter Street Center, the red-brick buildings along Front Street, the new luxury condos rising up in the old coal pocket, and the stately old homes that once belonged to nineteenth-century shipbuilders and shipmasters. As the beauty of Long Reach flashed on the screen, a lilting soprano voice sang "Haul Away, Joe!" and that shanty music carried me to a different time. When the music suddenly stopped, I heard the narrator's voice, but it wasn't Anna.

"If my mother were alive today, I would ask her a lot of important questions that I never had a chance to ask. I would ask her why she never returned to Maine to live, because she longed for it. She used to tell stories about climbing the rocks on Fox Island, picking blueberries at her grandfather's farm, and taking ferry rides across the Kennebec. Sadly, my parents and I vacationed only once in Maine before my mother's passing. I remember we took a boat ride from Popham Beach to Seguin Island and hiked up a winding trail to tour the lighthouse and picnic on its front lawn. It was a sunny afternoon, so we didn't encounter any spirits from the dark side, but the old lighthouse keeper told us about the ghosts that haunted the island, and I was thrilled."

* * *

I kept my eyes fixed on the screen as a series of images revealed Bath's maritime history. I saw the burning of the Old South Church through the eyes of a painter, and I noted an osprey as it flew by the Doubling Point

Epilogue

Lighthouse. There was a virtual tour through a sea captain's house, and a portrait of Arthur Gannett. But my favorite image was the black-and-white photo of a schooner ready to be launched at the Goss and Sawyer Shipyard.

"Over the course of that enchanting summer, we took a guided tour of Bath Iron Works. My mom and dad seemed so happy to be surrounded by cutting-edge naval engineering and maritime history. Their obvious delight in everything nautical made them seem younger and much more fun-loving. Today, I can still see their playful smiles in my mind's eye, and I can still see the sun on my mother's face as she admired the boats on the Kennebec."

* * *

As I watched the mother of a decorated Navy Seal break a bottle of champagne over the bow of a ship named in her son's memory, I was struck by a wave of emotion. I blinked back tears as I listened to my own voice express my deepest thoughts.

"I was seventeen years old when my mother died. My dad told me that God had made her all well, that she could no longer feel pain, and that her ship had finally reached its home port. My father hoped those words would comfort me, but my mother had passed out of my sight, and I felt alone and adrift. On sky-blue days, I like to imagine that my mother's forever harbor looks like Long Reach because that was the place she used to describe when she told me bedtime stories. She had so many tales to tell about shipbuilders, sailors, shanty songs, and tall ships along the Kennebec. I asked her one night why she left Bath, and she said in a soft voice, 'I fell in love with a handsome navy man with broad shoulders and smiling eyes, and I decided to follow him.'"

* * *

A little over a year had passed since Anna had interviewed me about her grandmother's strong connection to

Bath. I remember we sat on the deck and talked for hours, and Anna recorded every word. There were moments when I could tell by the look on her face that she thought my story was too incredible, but truth is often stranger than fiction. On that hot summer day, I told Anna that Ty and I had found our dream house when we visited Bath in the middle of a snowstorm. It was only my second trip to the mid-coast of Maine. My first had been in 1959, when my parents and I spent a week at a rustic lodge in Phippsburg. I don't know why I waited so long to return, but when a realtor showed us the house on Washington Street, and I climbed its winding staircase to the second floor and saw the bedrooms with their pumpkin-pine floors and elegant fireplaces, I knew we would buy the house. It was the most impulsive decision Ty and I had ever made, and it was a good one.

On that snowy day, I felt the irresistible charm of an old house in the historic district of Bath. I didn't know it was once the home of my own great-grandfather, Captain Henry Goss; nor could I have imagined that my grandfather, Captain Thomas Goss, would return to his boyhood home and live there with his first wife and his first child. And much later, he would return again with his second wife and their only child, Stella Rose. From time to time, Anna had to stop the tape to process the unbelievable facts. It was an emotionally charged interview. When it was over, Anna was clearly pleased with my words, but I had no idea that she would use my voice to make Bath's history feel close and personal.

Over the course of twelve months, Anna had spoken to a score of Bath residents, and she had included a number of their stories in her film, but Stella Rose was the North Star. *The Mariners of Long Reach* showed the glory and heartbreak of Yankee shipbuilding through Stella's eyes. At the end of the film, I was surprised to hear Anna's voice posing a single question: "Why, after living all over the country, does Bath feel like home?" And my own voice answered without missing a beat: "It sounds crazy when I say it out loud, but I feel my mother's spirit here. I believe her love is still here. Like her father and *his* father, Stella Rose Goss was a brave Yankee. As a mariner's daughter, she joined the navy to see the world, and she enjoyed a daring life, but in the end she found her way home, and so did I."

When the lights came up, I had to blink a few times to wash the dreams and tears away, and then Seth Gray's booming voice startled me.

"Ladies and gentleman, I am proud to introduce Anna Malone, the talented filmmaker who brought *The Mariners of Long Reach* to life for all of us this evening!"

As Anna reached the podium, she was greeted with a standing ovation. Over the loud applause, I could hear someone hooting and hollering Anna's name. And when I turned around to look, I realized it was Jake. He was standing at the back of the hall, shamelessly professing his love for Anna and her work. When I looked back at the podium, I could tell by the stars in Anna's eyes that she could see only Jake.

Ty squeezed my hand and put his lips on my ear. "I'm definitely retiring from Loyola at the end of this school year. You're right about Bath. There's magic in this City of Ships, and I think it's good for us."

I put my arms around Ty and whispered back, "Everyone needs a little Bath light in their life. Welcome home!"

CREDITS

I gratefully acknowledge the following sources for the invaluable information they offered me about schooners, square-riggers and America's maritime history, especially the shipbuilders and shipmasters of Bath, Maine:

Live Yankees by W. H. Bunting (Tilbury House Publishers, Gardiner, Maine, and Maine Maritime Museum, Bath, Maine, May 2009).

A Maritime History of Bath, Maine, and the Kennebec River Region (two volumes) by William Avery Baker (Maine Research Society of Bath, 1973).

I also acknowledge the following sources for unforgettable lyrics:

"Simple Gifts." 1848; written by Joseph Brackett Jr.

"Ole Buttermilk Sky." Copyright © 1946 by Hoagy Carmichael and Jack Brooks. Used by permission of Hoagy Bix Carmichael.

"Cecilia." Copyright © 1969 by Paul Simon. Used by permission of the publisher, Paul Simon Music.

"Shenandoah." Nineteenth century; unknown author: loc.gov/creativity/Hampson/about_shenandoah.html.